The *Antelope* Co

"Spelbush?" Brelca said. "When we are outside, where do we go?"

Spelbush turned the question over in his mind. "I would have thought that the answer to that was plainly obvious," he said.

"It isn't to me," said Brelca.

"Me neither," said Fistram.

"First of all, we're going underneath this door. Then we'll cross the garden and go out through the gate." Spelbush said.

"We know that," said Brelca. "Out into the world of giants. But then where do we go?"

Spelbush had a sudden flash of inspiration. "Why, we head for the sea, of course," he said.

"The sea?" said Brelca, in amazement.

"On foot?" asked Fistram, horrified.

"Where else?" said Spelbush.

"But the sea is miles from here," said Fistram.

"Miles and miles," said Brelca. "It would take us months to get to the sea from here – years, perhaps."

Willis Hall

The *Antelope* Company At Large

Lions

First published in Great Britain 1987
by The Bodley Head Ltd
First published in Lions 1988
Reprinted August 1990

Lions is an imprint of
the Children's Division, part of
the Harper Collins Publishing Group,
8 Grafton Street, London W1X 3LA

Printed and bound in Great Britain by
William Collins Sons & Co. Ltd, Glasgow

1

The portly little Lilliputian seaman took several steps across the bare floorboards towards the centre of the empty Victorian nursery. "I, Spelbush Frelock," he began, raising a clenched but trembling fist, "do hereby claim this uninhabited dwelling-place and situate garden territories—"

"Shut up, Spelbush!" snapped his two companions in unison, as they followed close behind him.

"Every solitary stitch of clothing that I possess went off in the removal van this morning—apart from what I'm standing up in," said Brelca, the pretty girl-sailor of the trio.

"The cook cleared out the kitchen before she left," moaned Fistram, who was forever thinking about food. "There's not a morsel to eat in the house!"

"A plumstone for all the food in the world, Fistram," snorted Spelbush, the self-appointed leader of the Lilliputian expedition. "And another plumstone too, Brelca, for all your clothing!" He paused and glanced around the nursery which looked even larger than it had done before, now that all the furniture had been removed. "There's a world out there," he continued, trying to sound brave, "waiting to be conquered."

"I've had enough of conquering," said Brelca, sadly.

"I've had more than enough adventures already to last me a lifetime," moaned Fistram.

The adventuring had begun for the little people over twelve months before. In the year 1899, the good ship *Antelope* had foundered and wrecked one stormy night off the English coast. But the *Antelope* was no ordinary ship. She had sailed all the way from Lilliput with a crew of tiny men and women who, by using Gulliver's maps and log-books and papers, had managed to re-chart his course.

Alas, only three members of that entire crew had survived the shipwreck.

Spelbush, Brelca and Fistram had been found on the seashore next morning by two children.

Philippa and Gerald Garstanton were on holiday at the seaside with their grandfather. Their father was an officer in Queen Victoria's army and, at the time of our story, both their parents were away in India. In the absence of their mother and father, Gerald and Philippa were living with their grandfather, Ralph Garstanton, a portrait-photographer.

The children, keeping the secret of the Lilliputians to themselves, had taken the little people back to their grandfather's house at the end of their holiday. The tiny folk had set up home in the dolls' house in the children's nursery on the top floor.

Only two other people knew of the existence of the Lilliputians. Harwell Mincing was a wicked fairground showman who, with the aid of his sister, Sarah, meant to capture the little people and put them on display in cages.

The Garstanton children, with the help of the little people themselves, had so far managed to defeat the plots

2

and schemes of the cruel Mincings. But the day had dawned when the Garstantons had moved on.

The children were to be reunited with their parents who were coming back to England. Grandfather Garstanton was moving off to retirement in the country. By accident however, in the move, the Lilliputians had been left behind in the empty house. The future now looked very bleak for the three tiny sailor-folk who found themselves stranded, high and dry, in a world of giants, without a friend to help them.

"Listen!" said Brelca, holding up a forefinger as her eyes darted over and around the empty floorboards that seemed to stretch away for ever.

Her companions both stood still.

"I can't hear anything," said Spelbush.

"Nor I," whispered Fistram.

"Me neither," said Brelca. "Doesn't the house seem empty now that the children have gone?"

"That's probably because it *is* empty," replied Spelbush in some irritation. "Which is why we have to move on—and the sooner we're on our way, the better."

Spelbush set off again towards the nursery door which, fortunately, had been left ajar. Before long, they were out on the top landing and looking down through the banisters. The stair carpet had been taken up and the bare wooden stairs that led down to the hall looked steep and perilously dangerous.

"Do we *have* to be so hasty?" asked Fistram, blinking as he gazed down. "Why don't we wait and see what the next people are like who move into the house? They might have children who are as pleasant as Gerald and Philippa."

"That's true—they might be richer than the last ones too," said Brelca who, it has to be admitted, could be something of a snob. "They might even be quite *grand* children," she added.

"Do you really think so?" asked Fistram, intrigued at the thought.

"I don't see why not," said Brelca, with a shrug. "They might even own one of those fashionable dolls' houses— like the one we saw in that catalogue the last children had just before Christmas. With *real* doors—and stairs."

One of the problems about living in the Garstanton dolls' house had been that not one of its doors actually opened or shut. They were all pretend doors painted on to the walls. Nor was there a staircase. The only way the little people had been able to get from one floor to the other was to ask the children to lift them up or down.

Fistram was even more cheered by Brelca's suggestion.

"You don't suppose they might own a toy fort?" he asked, excitedly. "I wouldn't mind living in a toy fort for a change. One with a drawbridge that went up and down. A big fort full of shiny toy soldiers?"

"The next people who come to live here, Fistram, might not have any children at all, have you considered that?" said Spelbush. "They might have cats instead. Or dogs. Big dogs with jaws that go up and down—and sharp, shiny, pointed teeth." He paused and made biting movements with his fingers and thumbs in front of Fistram's nose. "Woof-woof!" he said, and, "Snap-snap!"

"I don't know what we're hanging about here for," said Fistram, swallowing hard. "I think it's high time we looked for somewhere else to live."

So, for once, it was Fistram who led the way as the three

4

set off down the stairs.

But, although the little people did not know it, a far graver danger lay in wait for them outside the empty house than anything within it. In the shelter of a poulterer's shop doorway across the street, two sinister figures were keeping watch on the photographer's shop with the "FOR SALE" sign in the window. Both were tall and thin and dressed from head to foot in black. One was female and the other male. It was the woman who was the first to speak.

"And how can you be sure, brother," grumbled Sarah Mincing, "that your fairy folk have not packed their belongings too—and gone off to live in some mushroom in a fairy dell?"

Harwell Mincing's head twitched impatiently on his scrawny neck and he ran a finger round the inside of his grubby, starched shirt collar. "For the last time, sister, they are not fairy folk!" he snorted. "They are human beings, exactly the same as you or I."

"Human beings eight inches tall?" sniffed Sarah, who had always doubted the existence of the Lilliputians.

"*Yes!* And I *know* that they are in that house still. I was here this morning when the removal van left. The cunning creatures did not go off inside it, Sarah, I can swear to that. Confound it, I helped to load the wretched vehicle."

Harwell, for once, was telling the truth.

He had managed to bribe one of the removal men to let him take his place that morning. He had carefully searched every single piece of furniture as it was loaded on to the van. In fact, it had been Harwell's presence that caused the confusion which resulted in the little people being left behind.

But Sarah was still not convinced.

5

"Supposing what you say is true," she began, doubtfully, "and these little creatures do exist and they *are* in there still—"

"They do! They are!" exclaimed Harwell, excitedly.

"Even so, Harwell, we can't stand outside and watch the house for ever."

Harwell tapped the side of his nose with a long and bony forefinger. "I shall think of something, Sarah," he said, craftily. "In the meanwhile, we shall stand here and remain unobtrusive. The main thing is to let no one become aware of our presence . . ." His voice trailed off as he realized that someone had already seen him and his sister skulking in the doorway.

"Polish yer boots up for you, mister?"

The voice came from a small, ragged, fair-haired lad, who was gazing up at them. His name was Ernest Henshaw. He was ten years old and he carried a wooden box, complete with handle, which contained shoe-cleaning rags and polishes and brushes.

"Begone, boy!" snarled Harwell.

"Go on, mister," pleaded the lad. "Let me clean yer boots—I'll polish them that bright you'll be able to see yer face in 'em. It'll only cost a farthing."

"A farthing, you ragamuffin?" snapped Sarah, goaded by the very mention of money. "Do we look as if we are made of farthings? Do you think that farthings grow on trees?"

"No, missis," said the boy, staring up into their scowling faces.

"You heard me, you little cur," said Harwell. "Be off with you!"

"Please, mister," the lad persisted. "I've not earned

anything all morning. If I don't take something 'ome with me, I'll get my ears belted."

Harwell lunged forward and grabbed the boot black by the scruff of his neck. "If you don't take yourself off, this instant, ruffian," he growled. "I shall belt your ears myself—and have you put in charge for vagrancy!"

"Is he being a bother to you, sir?"

Harwell turned to look into the wrinkled face of an old woman, dressed in filthy rags, who had approached them from the opposite direction.

"What have I told you, Ernie 'enshaw," she scolded, "about pestering folk—especially toffs?" With which, she snatched the lad from Harwell by his coat collar and shook him as fiercely as a bull terrier might shake a rat. "It's the only language he understands, ma'am," the old woman said to Sarah as Ernest's head jerked violently from side to side.

"Ouch!" he groaned. "That hurts!"

"It's meant to hurt!" the old woman cried, shaking him all the harder.

Harwell Mincing glanced anxiously up and down the street, aware of the interest that was being shown by passers by. This wouldn't do at all, he told himself. The intention had been for him and Sarah *not* to get themselves noticed.

"If this urchin belongs to you, old crone," he barked at the old woman, "I'll thank you to take him home and punish him there—not here in public."

"He's mine all right, sir," said the old woman in wheedling tones. "Although there's many and many the time that I wished he wasn't—and there, that's his own grandmother saying it, as shouldn't. But *look* at him, sir and lady! He wears his clothes out faster than a pitman, and he has an appetite like a pitman's donkey. And look at his

7

shirt. You wouldn't think from the state it's in that I'd spent half last night a-washing and an-ironing of it, would you?"

Sarah was forced to agree with the old woman—although she didn't say as much. But certainly the shirt did *not* look as if it had been laundered the previous night. In fact, Sarah told herself, she would have been surprised to learn that any of the urchin's clothes had so much as *seen* a wash-tub in the past twelve months.

While Sarah Mincing was turning these thoughts over in her mind, the old woman had taken a fresh grip on the young lad's collar. Once again, she was jerking him fiercely to and fro, while at the same time fetching him several blows across the back of his head with her free hand.

"Ow!" yelled Ernest. "Gerroff!" he cried.

"Don't you say 'Geroff' to me!" ranted the old woman. "Don't you tell me to 'Geroff', my lad, or I'll knock you into the middle of next week!" At which point, she laid off the punishment for a while and, turning back to the Mincings, spoke again in her smarmy voice. "And that's how he speaks to his own grandmother, sir and lady. His very own grandmother what frets and worries how to fill his platter. If someone was to give me a penny, I could happen buy him a little meat-pie to fill his little belly, bless his heart."

"Push off, old crone," snapped Harwell. "We don't encourage beggars."

But Sarah, it seemed, had other ideas.

"Give her something," she whispered to her brother.

"What?" exclaimed Harwell in surprise, for he had never considered generosity one of his sister's virtues.

"Give her something!" Sarah hissed again. As she spoke,

8

she nodded across the street to where a constable was proceeding on his beat. "We don't want the police prying into our business. Give her something to get rid of her— *quickly*!"

Harwell, spotting the danger for the first time, fished all the loose change out of his pocket and examined the coins in the palm of his hand, looking for the least valuable one. But Sarah, acting quickly, snatched two of the coins from the collection and pressed them into the old woman's fist.

"Here's twopence, old drudge," she said.

"Twopence!" gasped the old woman, unable to believe her luck.

Sarah nodded. "Given as a gesture of our approval at the way you are bringing up that child—there is nothing like firm discipline to mould a lad's character."

"Twopence!" the old woman repeated, joyfully. "Oh, thank you, sir! Oh, thank you, lady! Just look at that, Ernie 'enshaw—a whole two pennies to ourselves! Why we must run to the ale-house right away and tell your grandad of this good fortune! He'll need to celebrate the news, I fancy, with a tankard of ale. And happen there'll be a glass of gin for me as well. God bless you both, kind sir and lady!"

Then taking a firm grip of the boy's ear, she led him off along the street. Not a moment too soon, it seemed, for the constable had paused on the other side of the street, directly opposite to where Sarah and Harwell stood, and was looking at them suspiciously. The Mincings favoured the policeman with their most innocent smiles.

"Walk away, sister," Harwell hissed through clenched teeth. "We'll come back later when the coast is clear."

They set off along the street, trying to look as if they were the most law-abiding citizens in the world.

Meanwhile, inside the empty house, the three little people had managed to climb all the way down the uncarpeted stairs. They were now standing in the hall, gazing up at the front door which was firmly shut.

"Do you suppose it's locked?" asked Fistram.

"Of course it's locked," said Spelbush. "You don't think they'd go off for good and leave the front door open, surely—for any passing giant to walk inside?"

"Locked or unlocked," said Brelca, "it makes no difference to us—*we* can't reach up and open it either way."

Fistram gulped and his eyes wandered round the bare floorboards and the empty walls.

Only a day ago, the house had seemed such a warm and friendly and *busy* place. There had been the children's laughter echoing round the rooms. There had been the clatter of Millie the housemaid's boots as she ran up and down the stairs. There had been the warm, inviting cooking smells coming up from the kitchen. There had been the comings and goings of customers to and from Mr Garstanton's studio. Now, all these things were gone. Bare of furniture and carpets, the house was still and silent as a tomb—and the three Lilliputians were locked inside it!

"We're incarcerated without food or warmth," said Fistram, in a nervous voice. "We're doomed, Spelbush."

"Plumstones, Fistram. We're not doomed at all," replied Spelbush, trying to sound more confident than he really felt. "The new owners will be arriving soon, won't they, Brelca?" he added, less surely.

"Perhaps."

"Perhaps not either," said Fistram, unhappily. "For all you know, Spelbush, the new owners might not come here for months—by which time we'll have starved to death."

"There's more than one way out of here," said Spelbush. "There's a gap big enough for us to crawl under at the bottom of the wash-house door—cook was always complaining about the draught blowing through."

"How do we get into the wash-house though?" asked Fistram.

"Simple," replied Spelbush. "Through the kitchen door."

Brelca shook her head and pointed along the hall. "We can't get into the kitchen," she said. "The kitchen door's shut tight like this one."

Fistram began to tremble all over. His knees knocked together. "I told you we were doomed!" he wailed.

Brelca turned and set off back the way they had come, towards the stairs. "Follow me!" she said.

"Follow you where to?" demanded Spelbush.

"Don't ask questions. Do you want to get out of here, or don't you?"

Spelbush and Fistram exchanged a mystified glance and then, without a word, set out after Brelca.

Minutes later, they had clambered back up the first flight of stairs and entered the dining room, which stood as bare and silent as every other room in the house.

"What now?" asked Spelbush.

"There—that's our escape route down to the kitchen," said Brelca, pointing across at the dumb-waiter which was resting, where it had last been used, at the hatchway in the dining-room wall.

"The dumb-waiter?" said Fistram. "But we could never move it."

"And even if we could move it," added Spelbush, gloomily, "there's no way that we could climb up to it."

II

"I'm not suggesting that we move it—or climb up to it," said Brelca. "Come along."

And now she led them across the polished floorboards and into a shadowy corner of the room beneath the dumb-waiter's hatch. Brelca pointed at a mouse-hole in the skirting board.

"Through there," she said. "I hid in there once from the maid. One afternoon while you pair were snoring your heads off in the nursery window-box."

"Us?" exclaimed Fistram.

"Nonsense!" said Spelbush. "I never snore."

"You did on that occasion," replied Brelca. "It was that time when you both guzzled all the sherry out of the bottom of the trifle bowl."

Spelbush and Fistram looked at one another, embarrassed, and decided not to pursue the subject. They turned their attention back to the mouse-hole instead.

"Is it . . . is it safe through there?" asked Fistram.

"I shouldn't think so for a moment," said Brelca, cheerfully. "Come on!"

With Brelca leading the way again, they crept on hands and knees through the hole which brought them out on to a narrow ledge bordering the dumb-waiter's shaft. It was dark inside the shaft. The shadowy figure of a huge mouse scuttled ahead of them along the ledge and disappeared through another hole in the brickwork.

They got to their feet, slowly, keeping as close to the wall as possible.

"Don't look down," said Brelca.

But she spoke too late. Fistram was already peering over the edge. He could not see the bottom. The shaft seemed to stretch away for ever, ending in total blackness. Fistram swallowed hard and blinked. In his anxiety he almost lost his balance and, for one nail-biting moment, he teetered on the very brink of the ledge. Spelbush and Brelca grabbed at his trousers and yanked him back to safety in the nick of time.

Keeping their backs tight up against the wall, the three Lilliputians edged their way carefully around the rim of the shaft. At one point, Brelca had to take out her knife and hack a way through a disused spider's web before they could continue.

After some minutes, they arrived at the ropes which controlled the dumb-waiter. The ropes were near enough to the ledge for the little people to be able to reach out and grab hold. Brelca's intention was suddenly clear.

"Do you mean us to climb down there?" asked Spelbush, nervously, looking down the length of rope which disappeared into the darkness below.

"You're not afraid, are you?" asked Brelca.

Spelbush stuck out his chest. "I am Spelbush Frelock, adventurer and explorer," announced the little fellow, pompously. "I would have you know, Brelca, that I do not know the meaning of fear. I do, however, recognize the need for caution . . ." He paused and then added in a small voice, "Isn't there another way down?"

"Not if you want to get into the kitchen," said Brelca. She reached out, took a firm hold on one of the ropes, swung her feet out and wrapped them around it. Hand-over-hand, the Lilliputian girl-sailor began to lower herself down the shaft.

Up on the narrow ledge, her two companions watched her. "Come on!" she called. "It's as easy as falling off a log!"

"Or falling off a rope," Spelbush muttered uneasily to Fistram. "Oh well," he continued with a shrug. "If she can do it, I suppose we can too." With which, he reached out and took hold of the rope. Spelbush had just started to follow in Brelca's wake when Fistram called down to him. "It's no good, Spelbush. I *am* afraid. I can't do it."

"Yes, you can, Fistram. If you *try*. Reach for the rope, take hold, and close your eyes."

"I *can't*. I just can't. I never did have much of a head for heights. You two go on. I'll stay here."

"Suit yourself," called Spelbush, nodding up at the shaft just above where Fistram stood hovering uncertainly. "At least you won't be short of company."

Fistram glanced upwards. The spider's web that Brelca had hacked through was not uninhabited after all. A huge black spider was picking its way down the brickwork directly above Fistram's head.

Fistram let out a yell of fear and made an immediate grab for the rope.

A moment later, all three Lilliputians were inching their way down the rope that led to the kitchen and, they hoped, to freedom.

2

"I don't suppose it occurred to you to consider how we were going to get down from here?" asked Spelbush.

Brelca shook her head.

"No, it wouldn't have done," snapped Spelbush.

The three little people, having successfully made their way down the rope, were standing on the edge of the dumb-waiter's hatch in the kitchen. Spelbush and Brelca were gazing gloomily at the stone-flagged kitchen floor below. It seemed an awfully long way away.

It was Fistram's turn to take the initiative. "There are times, you know," he said, "when intelligence comes in more useful than fine words and sheer bravado."

Brelca and Spelbush looked where Fistram was pointing. An old pair of kitchen-scales, left behind by Cook, hung on the wall close by the hatch.

Brelca and Spelbush raised their eyebrows and shrugged their shoulders, unable to guess at Fistram's plan.

"Watch this!"

Fistram leapt off the ledge on to one of the scales' pans. His weight caused the pan to travel gently downwards, far enough to allow him to jump nimbly off and safely on to the floor. He looked up and waved to his companions.

"Well done, Fistram!" Brelca called down.

Spelbush kept his mouth shut and pretended to be

unimpressed but, secretly, he was wishing that he had thought of it first.

Once Fistram's weight was off the scales, the pan rose to its previous position. Brelca, following Fistram's example, was next to use the "lift" down to the floor.

Spelbush was last to go. But he, alas, weighed almost twice as much as the other two put together. When he jumped on to the scales the pan shot down so quickly that it hit the ground with a bump and deposited Spelbush heavily on the stone floor. Spelbush got to his feet gingerly rubbing his backside. He looked at his two companions suspiciously. Both of them, he was almost sure, were trying hard not to laugh.

"I came down quickly on purpose, you know," he said. "I felt, as leader of this expedition, that it was my duty to test that apparatus at top speed—in case we ever encountered another of those contraptions and we needed to make a hasty getaway . . ." His voice trailed off. It was plain to him that neither Fistram nor Brelca believed a word of what he was saying. They were both grinning. "Well, don't just stand there!" he snapped. "Follow me!"

With Spelbush leading, the three Lilliputians made their way across the kitchen floor into the wash-house.

Spelbush had been right. There was a gap at the bottom of the wash-house door big enough for them to get through. Spelbush was about to squeeze his fat little frame underneath the door when Brelca put out a hand to detain him.

"Spelbush," she said. "When we *are* outside, where do we go then?"

Spelbush turned the question over in his mind. He was not going to admit that he had not yet given the matter a moment's consideration. "I would have thought that the answer was plainly obvious," he said at last.

"It isn't to me," said Brelca.

"Me neither," said Fistram.

"Do I have to explain everything to you two before we do it?" asked Spelbush.

"Yes, please," they replied in unison.

"Don't you trust me at all?"

"No, we don't."

"I see. Very well then, if that's your attitude," said Spelbush, rather hurt, "I'll tell you *exactly* what my plan is. First of all, we're going underneath this door. That will take us out into the garden. Then we'll cross the garden and go out through the gate."

"We know that," said Brelca. "Out into the world of giants. But then where do we go?"

"Well, we . . . we . . . we . . ."

"Go on, Spelbush," said Fistram. "Tell us."

Spelbush had a sudden flash of inspiration. "Why, we head for the sea, of course," he said.

"The *sea*?" said Brelca, in amazement.

"On *foot*?" asked Fistram, horrified.

"Where else?" said Spelbush, delighted at his own ingenuity.

It *was* a truly magnificent plan. Audaciously simple as a proposition—but one that would prove breathtakingly daring in its execution.

"But the sea is miles away from here," said Fistram.

"Miles and miles," said Brelca. "*Giants*' miles, as well. It would take us months to get to the sea from here—years, perhaps."

"All the same, if we are ever going to get back home to Lilliput, we will only do it by crossing the oceans," said

Spelbush. "And to achieve that, we must first get to the coast—even if it takes for ever. Shipmates, we three are about to set out on an epic journey. In the years to come, scholars and poets will write about our brave deeds." He paused and glanced around the wash-house. "Take your last look at these walls, shipmates," he advised, "for this house has given us good shelter and you will not set eyes on it again."

Brelca and Fistram fell silent, feeling the solemnity of the moment.

"Follow me!" cried Spelbush and, so saying, he rolled his tubby little body through the gap between the door and the floor. He was followed instantly by his two companions.

Once outside in the wide world of the garden, Spelbush drew his sword and waved it twice above his head. "The first footstep is always the most important," he declared. "Or, as our honoured countryman and folk-hero, Telbut Parba, said as he set foot on the alien shores of Rubriganda: 'It's a small step for a Lilliputian, but a giant leap for Lilliput!' *Forward!*"

And Spelbush took his first determined steps across the garden, followed by Fistram and Brelca.

They had barely covered half a metre however, when they spotted a huge mongrel dog standing just inside the open garden gate. Seeing the little people, the dog bared its teeth and let out a low growl.

"R-r-r-r-retreat!" stammered Spelbush, turning on his heels as he spoke and making a beeline for the wash-house door.

Seconds later, the three little people were back inside the wash-house.

After Spelbush had caught his breath he wiped his brow,

recovered his composure and looked around at the white-washed walls as if he had never seen them before.

"Well now, shipmates, this looks as good a place as any to pitch our camp," he said. "We'll set up base in the cupboard underneath the sink—and re-think our tactics after dark."

Fistram and Brelca exchanged a glum look. There was no need for words. They shared the same thought. It seemed as if they would be trapped in the empty house for some time yet. With their heads bowed despondently, they trudged after Spelbush as he led the way back into the kitchen.

That night, in the cupboard under the kitchen sink, the three Lilliputians huddled for warmth round the flickering flame of a candle-stub they had discovered. The moon shone through the kitchen window, casting a pale light on the half-open cupboard door. Brelca and Spelbush were sitting on a worn-out scrubbing-brush while Fistram was on his feet, chomping on a piece of cheese so big that he needed both his hands to hold it.

"Have some," said Fistram, offering the hunk of cheese.

"No, thank you!" Spelbush and Brelca spoke together as they glanced at the empty mousetrap in the corner of the cupboard.

An owl hooted in the nearby park and Spelbush shivered.

"It's been dark for hours now, Spelbush," said Brelca.

"I know."

"I thought that we were going to re-think our tactics once it got dark?"

"I *am* re-thinking our tactics," said Spelbush, huffily. The owl hooted again and Spelbush rubbed his hands together between his knees. "Tactically speaking," he said, "I think we're better off where we are."

"If we're to shelter from owls by night and from stray dogs during daylight hours, I don't see us ever travelling very far," said Brelca, wisely.

"Do you know something," said Spelbush, choosing to ignore Brelca's words, "I never quite realized how useful those children were—we're going to miss them."

"In some ways they were useful, yes," said Brelca. "On the other hand, there were times when they were . . . well . . . childish."

"They were extremely useful at assisting us in getting from one place to another," said Spelbush.

"We'll be much better off without them," replied Brelca, firmly, "once we've learnt to stand on our own two feet."

"I agree with Spelbush," said Fistram. "We *are* going to miss them. They were very good at getting us things to eat."

"Trust you, Fistram," mocked Brelca, "stomach first as always!"

"But it's the truth, Brelca!" replied Fistram. "We can't sit in this cupboard for ever—we'll starve to death."

"If it's got anything to do with you, Fistram," said Brelca, looking pointedly at the unbaited mousetrap, "the mice in here will perish from hunger long before you—"

"Ssshhh!" broke in Spelbush, holding a finger to his lips.

"What is it?" Fistram spluttered anxiously through another mouthful of cheese.

"I heard something."

"You're probably imagining things," said Brelca. "It wouldn't be the first time that—"

Her words were cut short by the sound of breaking glass

crashing on the stone-flagged floor.

"I didn't imagine that, did I?" whispered Spelbush.

They all three held their breath as they tiptoed to the cupboard door. They watched as a shadowy figure, perched outside on the window-sill, pushed a hand through a broken pane of glass and fumbled with the window-catch. A moment later, the window was open and the intruder had eased itself into the room where it paused for a second, crouching on the window-ledge, and then sprang down on to the stone floor.

"Who can it be?" hissed Fistram, fearfully.

The Lilliputians had taken cover behind the cupboard door. They could hear the mysterious figure stumbling around in the half-dark of the moonlit kitchen.

"Harwell Mincing, who else?" replied Spelbush.

"We can't be sure that it's Mincing," whispered Brelca. "It might be a burglar."

"Nonsense, Brelca," said Spelbush. "Why should a burglar burgle an empty house? I'll wager a purseful of pearls to a plumstone that it's Harwell Mincing."

"What are we going to do, Spelbush?" hissed Fistram, nervously.

"Keep our heads," Spellbush replied. "If we keep quite still and don't make a sound, there's no reason why he should locate our hiding-place."

"None whatsoever," Brelca said. "Except, of course, that there's a candle burning to show him the way."

Spelbush glanced over his shoulder and gave a gasp of horror. He had completely forgotten about the candle-stump flickering on the floor. "Fistram, you put out the candle," he said. "I'll close the cupboard-door."

As Fistram moved to obey, Spelbush took hold of the

door with both his hands and pulled hard. The door began to close. At his back, he heard Fistram blowing.

"Help him, Brelca," urged Spelbush.

As Brelca went to Fistram's aid, Spelbush quailed at the sound of approaching footsteps. He felt someone take hold of and then tug the cupboard door from the other side.

A face gazed down at the Lilliputians in open-mouthed amazement. The face belonged to a small boy in ragged clothing who carried a boot-black's box underneath his arm.

"Who the heckers are you?" said Ernest Henshaw, for it was the same lad that had tangled with the Mincings in the street outside—although, of course, the little people did not know of that encounter.

Brelca was the first to recover herself. "It's a boy!" she said, stamping her foot in rage. "It's another boy! We've only just got rid of the last two children—and now another one shows up. Oh, plumstones, how infuriating!"

Ernest poked a finger towards Spelbush's chest. He could scarcely believe what his eyes could see and he wanted to touch one of the little people to prove that they really existed. "Are you real, or has somebody made you up?" he asked.

Spelbush, having no wish to be prodded, moved back. "Of course we're real, boy," he said. "Do we *look* as if somebody had 'made us up'?"

Ernest shook his head, not knowing what to think. "I don't know what you are," he said. "I've never seen anybody as titchy as you lot. You look more like dolls than folk."

"*Titchy?*" repeated Brelca, crossly.

"Dolls!" exclaimed Fistram, taking offence.

Spelbush plucked up his courage. He put up his fists and weaved and danced around in front of Ernest's outstretched finger. "Don't poke your finger at me, boy—or you'll soon discover how real we are!" he said.

"That's telling him, Spelbush," said Brelca. "Take him on!"

"Black his eye for him, Spelbush," cried Fistram.

"Don't be stupid, Fistram," said Brelca. "He can't reach that high. Black his ankle, Spelbush!"

Spelbush continued to duck and dodge and occasionally jab his fists in the general direction of Ernest's finger. But the boy paid not the slightest attention.

"Where have you come from?" asked Ernest. "Have you always been that titchy or have you shrunk?"

"Shrunk! Shrunk indeed!" exclaimed Fistram, insulted.

"Don't let him talk to you like that, Spelbush!" cried Brelca. "Give it to him!"

"Yes! Punch him on the nose," called Fistram.

"He can't reach his nose either," Brelca pointed out. "Punch him on the shin, Spelbush!"

"Who do you belong to?" asked Ernest, still disregarding Spelbush's boxing antics.

Spelbush, realizing at last that he was getting nowhere, dropped his fists and stood still. "We don't 'belong' to anyone, boy," he said, puffing out his chest. "We're not bondsmen—we're sailors."

"We're Lilliputians," added Fistram.

"Lily-who?" asked Ernest, who had never heard of Gulliver or the land of Lilliput.

"Not only have we been landed with another child, but this time an ignorant one to boot!" snapped Brelca. "At least the last pair had some slight inkling of geography—

this one's a numbskull. Send him about his business, Spelbush."

"Don't be so hasty, Brelca," Spelbush advised. "Even though he is only a child, he could prove of *some* use to us."

"I agree with Spelbush," said Fistram. "He might even help us to escape from here."

"Nonsense," said Brelca, sharply. "He'd be nothing but trouble."

"Don't scoff at opportunity, Brelca," said Fistram. "Remember that the humble plumstone was once surrounded entirely by plum. That's a saying we have back home in Lilliput," he added, turning to Ernest.

"What does it mean?" asked the boy.

"None of your business," replied Fistram. Then, turning back to Brelca, he said, "This boy could even help us to survive."

Spelbush nodded, eagerly, and pointed at the boot-black box on the kitchen floor. "He could carry us around in that," he said.

"He could find food for us," said Fistram.

Brelca shook her head. "I absolutely refuse to be drawn into another situation like the last one. I am not going to be totally reliant on a child again—fetching and carrying me meagre helpings of milk and biscuits. No, thank you very much!"

"Hey, hey, hey!" Ernest broke in. He had so far listened silently while the little people discussed the various uses to which he might be put. But enough was enough. "I'm not fetching and carrying for nobody. I've got myself to look after. I've run away from home, I have," he added proudly.

"There! You see!" said Brelca, unimpressed. "Not only

a boy but a vagrant. He'd be much more trouble than he's worth."

"You're probably right," said Spelbush with a sigh. "He's probably been reported as missing to the police. We can't afford to get mixed up with anyone who is wanted by the law. Our paths lie in different directions, lad."

"We would be millstones around each other's necks," said Fistram.

"Suits me, titchies," said Ernest. "You go your way, I'll go mine. I only came in here for a night's shelter. First thing in the morning, I'm scarpering."

"Good luck to you, boy," said Spelbush.

"Sleep well, lad," added Fistram.

"Ta-ra," said Ernest, waving a hand at the three little people as they made their way back into the cupboard.

Once inside, Spelbush and Fistram together took hold of the cupboard door and pulled it shut. Brelca, meanwhile, set about constructing makeshift beds for them out of some discarded dishcloths and dusters she had found in the back of the cupboard. The candle still flickered in the centre of the cupboard floor.

"Leave it," said Spelbush, as Fistram made one last attempt at blowing it out. "It could turn colder in the night," Spelbush continued, "so we may have cause to be grateful for whatever warmth that candle affords us."

"I'm glad we're all agreed about the boy," said Brelca, settling herself on a dishcloth mattress and pulling a yellow-duster blanket up around her ears. "We will be better off on our own."

"I suppose you're right," said Fistram. "All the same, it would have been pleasant to have something to look forward to in the way of food—apart from mousetrap cheese."

"I hope we've made the right decision," said Spelbush. "I can't help feeling that we might have put him to some use."

On the other side of the cupboard door, Ernest had curled himself up in the shadows in a corner of the kitchen. He was using the boot-black box as a head-rest, making it a little softer with his cap which he had rolled up for a pillow. He was drowsy and on the edge of sleep when a lantern appeared outside the open window.

"Anyone in there?" called a voice.

Ernest drew further into the shadows.

Outside in the garden, a police constable peered through the window. In the darkness of the kitchen, he could just make out the faint glow of light that flickered behind a cupboard door under the sink.

"That's odd," Constable Culpepper muttered to himself. "City constabulary here!" he shouted in his loudest and most official voice. The policeman had been on his beat through the backstreets when he had spotted the broken window from the garden gate. "If there's a felon in there and he don't speak up, it'll be the worse for him when I *do* lay hands on him!" he called through the open window.

And so saying, Constable Culpepper placed his lantern on the window-sill and attempted to hoist himself up beside it. But the task of heaving his ample frame up on to the sill proved too difficult. He would have to find something to help him scramble through the window.

Inside the kitchen, Ernest listened as the constable moved off noisily through the shrubbery and around the side of the house.

The boy clambered to his feet and hurried across to the sink-cupboard where he tugged open the door. The little people had not heard the constable and were all three fast asleep on their temporary beds around the candle-flame.

"Hey! Titchies!" cried the boy. "Wake up—quick!"

"Go away," said Fistram, with a yawn.

"We're sound asleep," murmured Brelca, snuggling down on her dishcloth.

"I made our position crystal-clear, boy," said Spelbush, opening one eye. "Our decision is irreversible."

"Where can I hide?" demanded Ernest, urgently. "There's a copper outside in the garden. He'll run me in if he gets hold of me."

"That is entirely your own concern, young man," said Spelbush, closing the eye that he had opened.

"And yours," said Ernest. "It was your light he spotted through the window. I'll bet he's looking for a ladder now. He'll be back any minute—this cupboard is the first place that he'll search."

Spelbush needed no second bidding. He was out of bed and on his feet in an instant. "Quickly, you two!" he commanded his companions. "There's only one place we can hide—back to the dumb-waiter."

"What's a dumb-waiter?" asked Ernest, adding, "And is there room for me as well?"

The Lilliputians looked at Ernest and then at each other. They arrived at a decision.

Outside in the garden, Constable Culpepper had not managed to find a ladder. He had, however, come across a wheelbarrow which he decided would do just as well. He pushed the wheelbarrow through the shrubbery and then up-ended it underneath the open window. It was possible for him then to scramble up on to the window-sill from where he squeezed his fat frame through into the kitchen. He pulled in his lantern and then lowered himself on to the stone-flagged kitchen floor. The constable tiptoed across the floor and flung open the cupboard door under the kitchen sink. The cupboard was empty—except for the stub of a candle burning on the floor and a few dishcloths and dusters.

"Now why the hummers," muttered Culpepper to himself, "should somebody want to light a candle and then stick it in a cupboard? And what's more important—who was that somebody, that's what I would like to know!"

The policeman picked up the candle-stub, blew it out and then put it back where he had found it. He lifted his lantern high above his head so that it cast its beams into every shadowy corner of the room. But there was no one to be seen. He walked over to the door leading to the hall and tried the handle—but the door stayed firmly shut.

"Whoever it was," he told himself, "they didn't go out this way, that is a fact—the door is well and truly locked." Next, he crossed to the door which opened on to the wash-house and, once more, he lifted his lantern which lit up the whitewashed walls.

But the wash-house too was empty.

Constable Culpepper frowned. Funny, he thought, as he looked again around the empty kitchen. And then his glance fell on the dumb-waiter which was standing empty in the kitchen hatch.

"Ah-hah!" said Constable Culpepper triumphantly.

Swiftly, he walked over to the hatch and tugged on the rope that operated the dumb-waiter, sending it upwards in the direction of the dining room. Constable Culpepper thrust his lantern into the shaft and peered down. But the shaft was still and silent and as empty, it seemed, as the rest of the house.

"It would seem, Wilfred, as 'ow the birds 'ad flown before you got 'ere," Culpepper said to himself, returning to the window. "All that remains for you, my lad, is to go back to the station and tender your report." Then, "Whoops-a-daisy!" he wheezed as he wriggled his body through the window and out into the chill night air.

As Constable Culpepper's footsteps faded along the garden path, the ropes controlling the dumb-waiter began to move in the kitchen hatch. A moment later, the dumb-waiter itself rattled down. The rope was being operated by Ernest who, together with the three little people, was concealed on top of the dumb-waiter's shelves. Once level with the ledge in the hatchway, the boy jumped lightly to the floor. He lifted the Lilliputians down gently, one by one, and placed them on the moonlit flagstones.

"Thank you, boy," said Spelbush, gratefully.

"That's all right, Titchy," replied Ernest. "If it hadn't been for you three, showing me where to hide, that copper would have run me in for sure."

"And had it not been for your timely assistance in operating that contraption," said Fistram, nodding at the dumb-waiter, "he would have captured us three as well."

"We are all indebted to each other," said Brelca.

Spelbush glanced at each of his companions in turn then, having got their nodded approval, he turned back to Ernest. "It's possible, lad, that we might have been a trifle hasty earlier," he admitted. "If you would care to reconsider your own decision regarding throwing in your lot with

29

us, we three would be agreeable in allowing you to join our expedition."

"If you would take upon yourself the role of foraging for rations," said Fistram, hungrily.

"And while you're about it, you could also keep an eye open for additions to our wardrobe," said Brelca. "The little girl who used to live here had a doll that was just about my size and had a quite extensive range of clothes. Now that they've both moved on, I find myself with nothing at all to wear except what I'm standing up in."

It suddenly occurred to Ernest that it was probable these little people needed his help much more than he was in need of theirs. Indeed, what possible help could *they* offer *him*?

"I don't know whether I could get you food *and* clothes," the boy said, doubtfully. Perhaps his first instinct had been right. He would stand a far better chance in the world, surely, without having to fend for three tiny folk. He wrinkled his brow and scratched at his chin.

"Why not try it for a day or two?" suggested Spelbush, hastily. He had realized that the boy was having second thoughts.

"Yes," urged Fistram, "just give it a *try*—if you'd only help us to get food—clothes aren't *that* important."

Brelca glowered at Fistram and was about to pursue the argument, but Spelbush silenced her with a glance.

Ernest considered the matter carefully. He had felt very lonely only a short while ago. It would be worth joining up with these curious little people, he told himself, if only for the sake of their companionship.

"Oh, go on then," he said with a grin. "I suppose if I've got to scrounge grub for myself—it wouldn't harm to scrounge a bit more for you as well. I mean, it can't take much to feed anyone as small as you three."

Spelbush and Brelca looked at each other, but there was little to be gained, they silently agreed, in raising the subject of Fistram's appetite now. And Fistram was not likely to mention it. The boy would find out soon enough that satisfying Fistram's hunger was no easy matter.

"There is just one thing, boy," said Spelbush. "You will henceforth refrain from addressing us as 'titchies'. I am Spelbush Frelock, adventurer, explorer and official emissary at the court of his most noble majesty, Emperor Golbasto—"

"Oh, don't be pompous, Spelbush!" said Brelca, then, turning to the boy, she added, "I'm Brelca."

"I'm Fistram."

"My name's Ernie," said the boy. "Ernest Henshaw." Ernest shook hands with all three of his new-found travelling companions—or at least he put out the tip of his right little finger which they each took hold of, in turn, with both hands.

"I think," said Spelbush, when the introductions were over, "that we all ought to try and get some sleep—we have a hard day in front of us."

And so the three Lilliputians and the boy lay down again on the kitchen floor of the empty house. But this time the little people did not seek the safety of the cupboard under the sink. They curled up in the shadow of Ernest's body.

They were, after all, a company of friends.

3

Early the next morning, when the sun had barely climbed above the roof-tops, the garden gate creaked open and two unsmiling faces peered around it.

"Is it absolutely essential, Harwell, that I must be a party to your criminal activities?" said Miss Mincing. Sarah had been brought up as a religious child and there were still times when her deep-rooted beliefs clashed with her natural greed.

"If it is your wish to be partner to a fortune, sister, then the answer's 'yes'!" snapped Harwell, who was never troubled by a conscience.

"I sometimes wonder, brother, if your hell-bent thirst for self-destruction will not be satisfied until the pair of us are clothed in shameful raiment—myself in Holloway Women's Prison garb and you in a mad-house strait-jacket."

Harwell, who was carrying a carpet-bag, beckoned to Sarah to follow him. "I shall not be satisfied, Sarah," he said as he led the way up the garden path, "until the pair of us are living in the lap of shameless luxury—and in a place befitting that life-style: Royal Harrogate Spa or Eastbourne or Tunbridge Wells." They had arrived at the door of the wash-house and Harwell handed his sister the carpet-bag. "Hold that," he said.

As Sarah took a grip on the bag, Harwell eased it open and removed an ugly-looking crowbar—one such as a burglar might use for breaking and entering.

"I won't deign to ask where you acquired that monstrous article!" snapped Sarah.

Harwell had already discarded the crowbar for a set of skeleton-keys which he had also taken out of the carpet-bag.

"The same place that I acquired these, Sarah," he said. "From an old acquaintance in the ale-house. These should do the trick."

Sarah watched, disapprovingly, as her brother went to work, trying the skeleton-keys one by one in the lock on the wash-house door. "Supposing someone's inside?" she said.

"The house is empty, Sarah. The old goat of a photographer and his grandchildren are gone—how many times must I tell you that? The house is not yet sold to anyone. The only creatures inside these walls are the cunning mannikins I mean to get my hands on. There is nobody else to disturb us—"

"Good morning!" called a cheery voice from just behind them.

Sarah and Harwell spun round, aghast.

A red-faced man with a walrus moustache and wearing overalls had just come round the side of the house. "You won't need the keys," said the workman as Harwell guiltily tried to hide the set of skeleton-keys behind his back. "The door is open. I've unlocked it. You can walk straight in."

Sarah and Harwell Mincing were dumbfounded. They stood and stared at the workman, mouths agape.

"Don't mind me," continued the workman. "You are Mr and Mrs Evans, aren't you? You've come up from

33

Wales to look over the house?"

"Indeed to goodness, man, we are indeed, look you," said Harwell. He had put on many disguises in his attempts to capture the little people. He was more than ready to pretend to be a Welshman if it would suit his purpose. "I am Evan Evans from Aberystwyth," he continued in his curious Welsh accent. "And this is my good lady, Blodwyn. Travelled all the way through the valleys, isn't it, look you, by donkey-cart and steam-train, didn't we, Blod girl?"

Harwell dug his sister in the ribs with his elbow in an attempt to prompt her into reply.

Sarah's lips moved soundlessly for several seconds. She was not as eager as her brother to attempt imitations. "There's distance, isn't it, look you?" she managed at last.

The workman nodded, cheerfully. "Yes," he said. "The house agent told me to expect you sometime today. I've come round to mend the broken window. Somebody broke into the place last night."

"Broke in?" gasped Harwell, horrified.

The workman nodded. "And out again," he said. "Lucky the house was empty and there was nothing worth stealing inside—"

The workman had no chance to finish. Harwell had already tugged the wash-house door open and darted inside, dragging Sarah along with him. Once inside the kitchen, he gazed around.

"Why should anyone break into an empty house?" said Harwell, echoing Constable Culpepper's words. His glance fell on the open cupboard door beneath the sink and the stub of a candle on the cupboard floor. "That's why the wretch came in!" he cried, swooping on the candle-stub. "Because he saw a light. The crafty mannikins, curse them,

34

were concealed under the sink."

"And now they're gone, brother," said Sarah, bitterly. "And a common sneak-thief has hold of them. The game is over at last, it seems."

But Harwell had not given up by any means. He had spotted some boot-cleaning rags and brushes and tins of polish in a corner of the kitchen. Tossing the candle-stub aside he snatched them up. "Look here!" he cried. "What do you make of these?"

Sarah Mincing pursed her thin, mean lips as she peered at the objects that Harwell was holding under her nose. "Old rags for the main part, brother," she sniffed. "Rags and remnants of boot-blacking—"

"Boot-blacking!" Harwell repeated excitedly. "*Boot*-blacking. Ye gods, Sarah, does that not bring anything to mind?"

"Only Millie Lottersby."

"Who?"

"Millie Lottersby. That slovenly housemaid I once had in my employ. She went off to work for the photographer after he holidayed in my seaside boarding-house. She could lay on blacking that thick you would take her for a brick-layer with a trowel—the wasteful slattern."

"A curse on Millie Lottersby," snarled Harwell. "Aye, and a curse upon myself too for letting the boot-black pauper loose on the streets. I should have had him and his worthless hag of a grandmother cast into the workhouse when I had the opportunity."

"What pauper?" asked Sarah. "What worthless hag?"

"Yesterday morning, sister. The boot-black ragamuffin that we encountered. It was he that broke in here last night. I'm sure of it."

"How can you be sure of that?" scoffed Sarah.

"Confound it, Sarah, he was *here*! Will you refute the evidence that is before your eyes? These are *his* rags. This is his boot-blacking. He emptied that box of his on to the floor of this kitchen last night. Now why would he do a thing like that, do you imagine?"

"Because he is an idle little wretch with no wish to work for a living?" suggested Sarah.

"No," snapped Harwell, impatiently. "Because he needed the box for more valuable contents, Sarah. Something precious that he found in this room. The crafty creatures themselves. I tell you, sister, all we have to do is find that boot-black brat and his box and we shall have the mannikins in our grasp at last—"

Harwell broke off as he realized that the workman they had met outside was now looking at them through the broken window.

"Is it to your liking then, Mr Evans, the house?" said the workman.

"Mind your own business, fellow, and attend to your work," said Harwell, curtly. "Come, Sarah—we have our own task to complete. We must needs search the streets until we find that boot-black."

He strode out of the kitchen, followed by his sister.

As the Mincings came out of the wash-house and swept down the garden path, they passed a greenhouse without giving it so much as a glance. But the three Lilliputians and the young boy who were hidden inside the greenhouse watched every step that Sarah and Harwell took until they were on the other side of the garden gate.

"Who do you say they are?" asked Ernest.

"The Mincings," said Spelbush.

"They've been trying to get their hands on us for months," said Fistram.

"We've always managed to get the better of them," said Brelca.

"So far," added Spelbush. "But now that there is nothing to detain us here, I suggest we put as much distance between ourselves and them as possible."

Ernest nodded. "Moving on from here suits me all right. I'm running away from home meself," he said. "Where do you want to go to? Burnley? Preston?" He had never travelled more than five miles from where he lived and Burnley and Preston sounded, to Ernest, like the other ends of the world.

"Further afield than that," said Spelbush.

"Eventually," said Fistram, "we mean to get back to Lilliput."

"But in order to do that," said Brelca, "we must first get to the sea."

"The sea!" gasped Ernest, softly. "That's miles and miles away is that. Is it as big as what they say? Does it go on for ever and ever?"

"It stretches all the way to Lilliput," said Brelca, solemnly.

"All eight oceans of it," added Fistram. "And we three must cross each one."

"What colour is it?" asked Ernest.

"Haven't you ever seen the sea, lad?" asked Spelbush.

Ernest shook his head, slowly. "I saw a picture of it once," he said. "This kid had got it in a book. But that were only a black-and-white drawing. I have heard tell that the sea is blue—then somebody else will tell you that it's green—or else greeny-grey, I've heard that too, with little

37

white foamy bits on top. What colour is it really?"

"It is all of those things and others beside," said Spelbush. "But you shall see them for yourself."

Ernest danced a little jig of joy on the greenhouse floor. "Hey—are we really going there?" he asked.

The Lilliputians nodded.

"Crikey Moses!" cried Ernest. "The fizzing sea!"

The boy's face lit up with glee and the little people also smiled, sharing his delight.

"In some ways, you know, I shall be quite sorry when we leave," said Fistram, pottering about in the window-box outside the nursery window. "This radish I've been cultivating is just about ready for pulling."

"Perhaps we could have it as a salad before we go?" suggested Brelca. "As a kind of goodbye feast?"

"One radish between four of us?" grumbled Ernest. "I don't call that much of a feast."

The boy sighed.

Several days had gone by since the morning in the greenhouse when the little people had announced that they intended to move on. But they were all three still in the empty house and the boy with them. They had got Ernest to take them up to the nursery, via the dumb-waiter, and, once there, had settled down to a life of leisure, doing nothing, it seemed, except letting the days drift by.

Ernest sighed again. It was all right for *them*, he told himself, sunbathing most of the time in the window-box. But he was the one who had to go out and forage for food: stealing an apple or an orange from a greengrocer's barrow, taking a loaf of bread when the baker's back was turned. He was the one who was expected to do *everything*.

38

"We look to your ingenuity, lad, to augment the spread," Spelbush had replied when Ernest had questioned the number of people that *one* radish would feed. "You could, for instance, go out and filch some salad-dressing," the Lilliputian had added, flicking at his beard with his finger-tips.

"Salad-dressing!" retorted Ernest, infuriated. "Where the eckers do you think I can get salad-dressing from?"

Brelca shrugged. "The last giant children who lived here were extremely good at foraging," she said.

"They were excellent," agreed Fistram (although he had rarely said so at the time). "They used to bring us all kinds of treats: cold rissoles and sausage-rolls—sometimes we even had a choice of pudding."

"Happen they did—but they weren't living in an empty house," Ernest snapped back.

"I suppose the child may have a point there, Fistram," said Brelca. "There is little to be gained by staying here—the sooner we make a start the better."

"When am I going to see the sea?" asked Ernest. "You did promise that I would."

"And so you shall, boy," said Spelbush. "But these things take time. Plans must be laid; routes must be planned; charts have to be—well—charted. My companions and myself are contemplating a voyage, lad, that is breathtaking in its magnitude. When the time is ripe, we shall be on our way. It is better that we lie low for the moment—at least until the Mincings have given up hanging about outside."

"How do you know they're still hanging about outside?" asked Ernest.

Spelbush thought for a moment before replying. "Instinct," he said at last. "They are out there, boy, make no

39

mistake about it—and up to no good too, that's certain fact—*Look out*!"

Out of the corner of his eye, Spelbush had spotted Fistram trying to tug the radish out of the earth with both hands. The radish had suddenly burst free, taking Fistram completely by surprise. He tumbled over on to his back and almost fell over the edge of the window-box down into the street three floors below.

Spelbush and Brelca rushed to help their companion to his feet. They brushed him down as he examined himself for bruises.

Ernest sighed for a third time. The subject of moving had been shelved again.

Several streets away, in the grubby smoke-filled atmosphere of his favourite ale-house, Harwell Mincing pushed his way through the usual throng of drunkards and ne'er-do-wells.

Harwell, who was carrying three drinks, made his way to an out-of-the-way corner table.

"A glass of soda water for you, sister," he said, putting one of the glasses down in front of Sarah, "and a gin for you, old woman."

The old woman that Harwell addressed was the very same that he and Sarah had encountered in the street some days before, the one who had declared herself to be Ernest's grandmother. It had taken some time for Harwell to track her down but he had stuck to the task. She had not been slow in accepting his invitation to a drink in the ale-house.

"There's your change, Sarah," he said, slipping some coins across the table. "Oh, and I took the liberty of purchasing a glass of medicinal Scotch whisky—my chest complaint would appear to have returned again, alas."

Sarah pursed her lips and Harwell turned back to the old woman, quickly changing the subject. "Is the gin to your liking, crone?"

"It's hard to say, sir," she croaked greedily, having already emptied her glass. "The first one allus goes down that quick I hardly gets the taste of it. It's my age d'y'see—I suffers something chronic from a parched throat."

Sarah, who did not approve of the ale-house or its customers, clicked her tongue disapprovingly.

"There'd be another in the glass for you, old biddy," said Harwell, "if you'll oblige us with a little information."

"We wish to speak to your grandson," said Sarah.

"Ah—that one!" wheezed the old woman. "Who wouldn't like a word with him? I'd like to get my hands on him myself, only it isn't possible. He's runned orff again."

"Runned orff?" repeated Harwell, not understanding.

"Runned away from 'ome, kind sir," said the old woman. "And not for the first time neither. Every time I find the little good-for-nothing work, he seeks to run away from it."

"Have you tried beating him regularly?" asked Sarah.

"Haven't I just! Why, I've thrashed him and better thrashed him. I've thrashed that lad until I've been blue in the face—to make a better child of him—but he's never once thanked me for it."

Sarah "tut-tutted". "They are all ungrateful brats are boys—without exception," she said. "They are widely known to be so."

"None more than that one," mumbled the old woman as she slipped into a monologue that came easily to her. "He's runned away from jobs that better boys would give their

41

eye-teeth for. Slaughterman's assistant in the knackers yard, he runned away from that. And had he persevered at it we could have had all the offal we could eat—but no, he has to run away from the task. And then there was the time I had the rare good fortune to get him fixed up as a 'andyman's assistant in the morgue. There's corpses comes in that morgue, mum, with that much money in their pockets it makes you wonder why they never clung on to life. Oh, there were rich pickings a-plenty to be had in that there morgue, but the idle little wretch runned orff from it!"

The old woman paused and jiggled her empty glass on the table in the hope that Harwell might replenish it. But Harwell made no attempt to do so and the old woman continued her complaining about her grandchild.

"That boy has runned orff from more employments than he's had mutton-bones off my plate to feed on. I haven't got the teeth myself, sir, any longer—so I sucks what meat I can off 'em first and then gives 'em to the lad, bless him, to chew on. And now see what thanks I gets for it—he's runned orff once again from his poor old grandmother what loves him more than life itself. The little swine, I'll swing for him when I gets my hands on him!"

"Quite so, quite so," said Harwell, producing a visiting-card from a waistcoat-pocket. "Take this," he went on, handing the card to the old woman, "and when the brat returns, bring him to that address and there'll be sixpence for you."

"Sixpence!" cried the old woman in amazement, clapping her bony hands together. "Why, if I only had half of that money now, I could happen get my shoes mended and then scour the streets for the little lamb."

"Nonsense, woman!" snapped Sarah. "It is having footwear that has proved the ruination of the lower classes. The heathen in far-off climes does not have shoes—no, nor a caring town council neither to give him pavements to walk on. Yet he can stay on his feet all day and fetch and carry for his Christian master. Be off with you and find the brat—and then you'll get all the reward that's coming to you."

Realizing that there would be no more gin nor cash forthcoming from the Mincings that day, the old woman pulled herself to her feet, muttering all the while. She was about to set off towards the door when Sarah spoke again.

"Wait! I will give you something on account," she said, fishing in her voluminous handbag and taking out a sheet of printed paper. "Here's a religious tract for you all about the hard-working heathen in foreign climes. There's a picture on it too. You shall be able to pin it on your wall and learn by his example. Good-day to you."

The old woman moved away, still cursing under her breath—but quietly enough for the Mincings not to notice.

"I don't doubt that she'll only use it to light the fire," said Sarah, turning to Harwell. "But if we don't show some sort of kindness towards the downtrodden, they will remain a burden on the parish and not achieve anything for themselves."

"And we are no further ourselves in achieving our goal," snarled Harwell. "Getting our hands on the boot-black boy and his accursed box."

Sarah shrugged her shoulders. Her long thin fingers twitched at her black coat. She was beginning to lose patience with the whole venture. "That brat, Harwell," she said, "is probably miles away from here by now—and your precious Cornish pixies with him."

"They are not Cornish pixies, Sarah!"

"Bearded gnomes then. One thing's for certain, as you have said yourself, they would not have remained an instant in that empty house once the photographer and his brood had left—how could those fairy folk have fended for themselves?"

Harwell, forced to concede the truth in what Sarah said, gnawed at his lower lip in his frustration.

But while Harwell Mincing agonized over his seeming bad fortune, there was much activity going on outside the empty house and shop. A horse-drawn removal van was parked outside and green-aproned removal men were carrying furniture in through the open door.

Inside the house, on the upper landing, the three Lilliputians and the runaway boy peered down through the banister rails at the to-ing and fro-ing on the lower floors.

"I tell you we're saved!" crowed Fistram with delight. "Someone's moving in. Just think of it—a cook installed in the kitchen again. The smell of new-baked bread coming from downstairs. I do hope this new one's a dab-hand with a pink blancmange."

Pink blancmange, it should be explained, was Fistram's favourite delicacy.

"Save your celebrations, Fistram," warned Brelca, "until we find out what this new family are like."

"It doesn't matter what they're like," trilled Fistram. "Pleasant or unpleasant, they've still got to eat. There's bound to be food for the taking in the kitchen once again."

"And a couple of cats too, perhaps?" Spelbush said. "Like a pair of sabre-toothed ginger tigers! Or a great gargantuan snarling dog!" Spelbush paused and made biting motions again with both hands in front of Fistram's nose.

"Woof-woof!" he said. "Snap-snap!"

"And even if there aren't any giant-sized animals waiting to tear us limb from limb," said Brelca, "how are we to get this food up from the kitchen?"

"That's my job," offered Ernest. "I'll bring the food up for you, like the last kids did."

"*You?*" said Brelca, scornfully. "The previous children *lived* here. They were allowed free access to the kitchen. I shouldn't think that the new cook will be particularly pleased if a total stranger walks into her kitchen and starts filling his pockets with food."

"Then he'll have to go downstairs and forage for us by night," said Fistram. "That's the simple answer. We'll hide up here by day and send him down when the household's fast asleep."

"Suits me," said Ernest.

"And there you pose another problem, Fistram," said Spelbush. "It's all very well you saying 'hide by day'—*we* can manage that very nicely—underneath a wardrobe or behind the skirting board. *Anywhere.* We can tuck ourselves into any nook or cranny, being our normal size. But how the plumstones can we possibly hide a great galumphing elephant like *him*?"

All three Lilliputians turned and stared accusingly at Ernest.

"I knew it!" stormed Brelca, stamping her foot. "You will both remember, I hope, that *I* was against taking him on board from the very beginning. I said then that he'd prove more trouble than he was worth. I say get rid of him now!" And, putting a hand up in the air, she added, "Let's take a vote on it."

"You are ungrateful, you three," said Ernest, angrily.

"Who's been going out and fetching food for you these last few days? How would you have managed without me?"

"It's true," said Spelbush, forced to agree. "And we did enter into an agreement with him. A Lilliputian's word is as good as his—" Spelbush broke off at the sound of footsteps coming upstairs.

The little people looked down through the banister rails again as Ernest ducked his head. They saw that two of the removal men were slowly moving up to the top landing carrying a cumbersome piece of furniture between them.

"Run for it!" hissed Fistram.

"Hide!" whispered Spelbush.

Ernest and the Lilliputians turned and fled along the landing. They ran into the empty nursery. There was a cardboard box in a corner of the room. It had once contained a set of toy soldiers but now it was empty.

"In there!" said Brelca, leading the way into the box which was standing on its side.

Fistram and Spelbush were quick to follow her.

In the excitement of the moment, Spelbush beckoned Ernest to follow him inside, forgetting that the box was just about big enough to hide one of Ernest's feet. The boy stood gazing down unhappily at the three little people inside the box. They could all hear the shuffle of the removal men's feet as they edged the piece of furniture along the upper landing.

"Don't just stand there, boy," wailed Fistram. "You'll give us all away!"

"Hide yourself!" hissed Spelbush.

"Hide *where*?" demanded Ernest, looking hopelessly round the room.

On the landing outside, the two removal men inched the

furniture nearer towards the nursery.

"In there, I imagine, Radleigh," said one of them, nodding towards the partly open door.

Radleigh, who was walking backwards holding up one end of the piece of furniture, glanced over his shoulder. "Hang on, Sumner," he said. "Put it down and I'll push the door wide open."

They lowered the furniture to the floor and Radleigh stretched out a hand towards the door handle. One gentle push and Ernest would be revealed.

"Sumner! Radleigh!" A voice called up from below.

The two removal men looked down over the banister rail. Their foreman was standing, hands on hips, looking up at them from the landing below.

"Did you want us, Mr Fletcher?" asked Sumner.

"I did indeed!" growled the foreman. "Would you mind defining for me that article of furniture you've carried up there?"

Sumner and Radleigh turned as one and studied the piece in question.

"It's a sideboard, Mr Fletcher," said Radleigh.

"It's Georgian," added Sumner, who wore a bowler hat with a dent in it.

"Oh, is it just? A Georgian sideboard, no less!" replied the foreman, gazing fiercely up at them. "You see a lot of them in bedrooms, do you? Georgian sideboards?"

Sumner and Radleigh looked at one another and scratched their heads.

"No, Mr Fletcher," said Radleigh.

"They mostly turn up in parlours, Mr Fletcher," added Sumner.

The foreman sighed and shook his head impatiently. "The

47

trouble with you two is that you never read your dockets. It's all set down for you where everything has got to go. 'Second floor: nursery and spare bedroom— please leave clear.' It's plain enough, surely to goodness? This here's the parlour down here, where your Georgian sideboard is expected. Fetch it down at once!"

"Yes, Mr Fletcher," said the removal men as one. Then, after spitting on their hands, they picked up the sideboard and set off back the way they had come.

Inside the nursery, the three Lilliputians walked out of the cardboard box and rejoined Ernest.

"Did you hear that, Spelbush?" asked Fistram. "No furniture in the nursery."

"What of it?"

"No furniture in the nursery means that there aren't any children in this new family."

"That's something to be thankful for! One stupid boy's enough to cope with at the moment," said Brelca, looking up at Ernest and rudely poking her tongue out at him.

"I wonder what kind of people they'll be, the ones that have bought this house?" asked Fistram. "You never know, they might even prove quite friendly towards us," he added.

Spelbush shook his head. "I doubt it, Fistram. They'll be giants—like all the rest of the inhabitants of this strange land. Amiability is hardly in the nature of the beast."

While the little people were talking, Ernest had been listening at the nursery door. "I think the new people have just arrived," he said. "I heard a woman's voice down-stairs."

Now that it was safe for Ernest and his three small companions to venture out once more, they went on to the

48

landing and looked down through the banister rails into the hall two floors below.

They were just in time to see the tops of two women's hats—although, from where they stood, it was impossible to see the faces underneath these bonnets—as they moved along the hall and into the kitchen. One of the hats was a particularly colourful creation decorated with a grand display of imitation fruit.

"That's odd," said Spelbush.

"What is?" asked Brelca.

"That hat with the entire harvest on top," said Spelbush. "I could have sworn that I've seen it before somewhere."

"Now that you come to mention it, Spelbush," said Fistram, "I'd willingly lay a plumstone to a pink blanc-mange that I've seen it before somewhere too."

The Lilliputians exchanged puzzled glances. Ernest shrugged his shoulders. *He* had certainly never seen the hat before.

4

Millie Lottersby pulled the hat-pin out of her best bonnet and sat down. "Well, I dunno, Cook, eh?" she said. "Talk about short and sweet! Short and sweet ain't in it, if you wants my opinion!"

"To-ing and fro-ing, to-ing and fro-ing! All this travelling to and fro ain't good for my corns," replied Cook, easing her aching limbs on to the only other chair in the kitchen. "Mind you, now that the coming and going's over," she added, glancing round the familiar walls with a satisfied smile, "I must say as I'm glad to be back in my dear old kitchen again."

"Me too!" agreed Millie. "'Ere, Cook—I will say this much: as long as I live, I shall never forget the looks on Master Gerald's and Miss Philippa's faces when they heard their pa and ma was coming back to England unexpected— all the way from India, no less!"

Gerald and Philippa Garstanton were the two children who, until about a week before, had lived in that very house with their grandfather, the photographer, Ralph Garstanton. And Millie and Cook had been his household servants.

"Is it today the kiddies' parents are sailing into port?" asked Cook. "It's all been such an excitement, I haven't been able to take it all in properly."

"That was yesterday, Cook. Leastways, it was yesterday

50

when the troopship docked at Liverpool—and Gawd bless every gallant soldier on 'er. And they're dis-em-watcher-ma-calling it today?"

"Disembowelling?" proffered Cook.

"Yer—well—something like that," said Millie, not at all sure that Cook had got *quite* the right word for coming off a ship. "Anyways, their grandad's taking the kiddies to meet their mum and dad off the boat today. And then Captain Garstanton's got 'is leave to come—so they're taking Master Gerald and Miss Philippa straight off on holiday."

"And the master will be coming home in time for his dinner," added Cook. "I only hope we get sorted out in here in time for me to have something ready for him to eat."

Millie shook her head and sighed. "I don't know how you're ever going to manage that, Cook," she said, glancing towards the empty larder. "There's not a thing in the house to offer him."

"I'll get a fire going under the oven, Millie, if you'll pop down to the shops and fetch me something back to tempt the master's appetite—a couple of nice chump chops, p'raps. I suppose he did the wisest thing, taking this house back off the market and coming here to live in it himself again? I mean, that house he took us out to in the country *would* have been much too big for him, wouldn't it, now that the kiddies have gone and he's on his own again?"

"Wisest thing for all concerned, Cook," said Millie, firmly nodding her head. "Not least of all, yours truly!" The housemaid paused and grinned. "'Ere—one look at all them cows standing around in all them fields, and I was ready to come back 'ere straight off! They didn't arf put the wind up me, Cook! Why, I never knowed cows was *that* big. I'd no more go near one of them than I'd go inside the lions' cage at London Zoo!"

While Millie was speaking, the removal foreman had walked into the room carrying a kitchen chair. He coughed politely, then, "Pardon me, miss?" he said.

"No sooner asked than granted," said Millie.

"Here's another of your kitchen chairs," said the foreman, putting the chair down. "Oh, and by the way," he added, pausing before going out again, "according to my instructions, there's nothing to be taken up to the nursery, on the top floor?"

"No, no more there ain't," said Cook.

"That's right," said Millie. "Now that the master's grandchildren aren't going to live here any longer, all their bits and pieces has been put in store—the nursery won't be used no more."

"So where do you want the dollies' house to go then?" asked the foreman.

Millie and Cook looked puzzled.

"What dollies' house is that?" asked Millie.

"The dollies' house isn't coming back here," said Cook.

"If that's the case," said the foreman, "perhaps you'll tell me what it is that's outside in the hall that's just come off the van this minute—and is standing out there now as large as life and twice as natural?"

Cook and Millie followed the foreman out into the hall. Sure enough, as he had said, the Garstanton children's dolls' house was standing in the middle of the hall. Through one of its windows they could also make out the dolls' house furniture, stacked in one of the rooms.

"Well, I never!" said Millie. "That's our dolls' house

right enough, is that! But 'ow's it managed to turn up here again?"

"Need you ask?" growled the foreman as Radleigh and Sumner walked in through the front door carrying between them a chest of drawers. "When you're at the mercy of a pair of chumps who've got no more sense than to carry a Georgian sideboard up to the top floor of a house? You're only lucky to have your dollies' house turn up anywhere at all!"

The workmen grinned sheepishly at their foreman as they set off upstairs with the chest of drawers.

"Well, it can't stay here, and that's a fact," said Millie, looking glumly at the dolls' house. "Whatever would the master say if he was to walk in and see it there?"

" 'Bless my soul', perhaps?" said a familiar voice behind them. "Or possibly, 'Well, I never!' or even 'Steady the Buffs!' "

Cook and Millie turned in surprise to discover that their employer, Mr Garstanton, had walked through the front door unnoticed and was looking down at the dolls' house.

"Why, Mr Garstanton, sir," said Millie, "we wasn't expectin' you 'ome till this evening!"

"And me with the kitchen all at sixes-and-sevens and not so much as a currant tea-cake in the bread-bowl!" said Cook.

"I'll slip my coat on right away, Cook, and run them errands for you," said Millie.

Cook and Millie scuttled off towards the kitchen.

"Good morrow, sir!" said the foreman, tipping his cap at Mr Garstanton. "New Century Pantechnicon Removals, at your service! Apologies for this little how-d'yer-do . . ." He gestured at the dolls' house. "I'll get my lads to convey it back on to the vehicle forthwith."

"Thank you, I'd be very much obliged," said Mr Garstanton, staring sadly at the dolls' house. It reminded him of days now past when the house had echoed to the laughter of his grandchildren. He was pleased for them, of course, now that their parents had returned from abroad—but he would miss them all the same. "Wait a minute," he said as the foreman moved towards the foot of the stairs.

"Yes, sir?"

"On second thoughts, now that it's in the house—ask your men to be kind enough to carry it up to the top floor."

"If that is your requirement, sir?"

"It is indeed. My grandchildren, I am sure, will be visiting me occasionally—it would be only right to have something in the house to occupy their leisure hours."

"No sooner said than done, sir," said the foreman.

Mr Garstanton, left alone, opened the front of the dolls' house and peered inside. Some of the more fragile pieces of dolls' house furniture had been wrapped in coloured tissue paper. Mr Garstanton unwrapped one of these. It was a tiny wash-stand. He turned the delicate piece of woodwork over in his hands. Then remembering happy times gone by, the photographer took out his handkerchief and blew his nose, hard.

"I know it ain't my place to speak, sir, an' I 'opes as 'ow you'll forgive me for venturing to do so . . ." Mr Garstanton turned to discover that Millie had re-entered the hall, now wearing her outdoor coat and carrying a shopping basket. "But you're going to miss not 'aving them kiddies around no more," she said. "Bless me if you ain't, sir, beggin' yer pardin, sir."

"Oh, nonsense! Nothing of the kind, Millie! Quite the

reverse in fact!" said Mr Garstanton, but his voice sounded a little too cheerful to be convincing. "It'll make a pleasant change not having 'em banging and clattering up and down the stairs all hours! Boot-prints all over the herbaceous borders! Toy soldiers down the back of the sofa! Doll's perambulator left on the landing for me to trip over! Continual din from the nursery. Miss 'em, Millie? Absolutely the opposite, eh, what? Tell you the truth—I'll be more than grateful for a quiet life!"

"Yes, sir. Very good, sir. Whatever you says, sir." But Millie was not at all taken in by her employer's pretended cheerfulness. "I'd best be off and run Cook's errands."

As the front door closed behind Millie, the smile faded from Mr Garstanton's face.

A moment later, the two removal men came down the stairs, picked up the dolls' house and, carrying it between them, set off for the top floor. Mr Garstanton watched them go and then, taking out his handkerchief, blew his nose again, harder than before.

Minutes later, the dolls' house was back in its rightful place and the removal men were on their way downstairs again. The little people and their boy companion crept out of the spare bedroom and tiptoed into the nursery where they all four stood gazing at the dolls' house in the centre of the floor.

"Home sweet home," said Brelca, simply.

"Or the nearest thing to it this side of eight oceans," said Fistram.

Spelbush was the first to pull himself together. "Don't stand there gawping at it, lad," he said to Ernest. "Open the front wall for us."

Ernest did as he was told. He stared wide-eyed at the

55

inside of the dolls' house. He had never had any toys of his own. He had never even seen anything like it. "Is it yours?" he asked. "Is it where you live?"

"It's ours to all intents and purposes," said Fistram. "We have an understanding with the previous owners on a rather loose arrangement."

"Come along, lad," said Spelbush. "Get on with it. If we three are to spend tonight inside our own four walls again, there's work to be done."

"Packages to be unwrapped," said Brelca, pointing at the pieces of furniture wrapped in tissue paper.

"Carpets to be laid," said Fistram.

"Curtains to be hung," said Brelca.

"All the furniture is to be arranged around the rooms," said Brelca.

"Hammocks to be slung," said Spelbush.

"That's what I'm really looking forward to," said Fistram, "after the boy has sorted out our living quarters and scavenged a four-square meal for us this evening—a good night's sleep in my own comfortable hammock again."

"Am I supposed to do *everything*?" asked Ernest.

"A goodly share," said Spelbush. "Giant's hands make light work."

"And I'm not a giant either!" snapped Ernest.

"That's what all you giants say," sniggered Brelca.

"Get on with it, boy, get on with it!" said Spelbush, testily. "The sooner we set this house to rights, the sooner we can sit down round a table and begin making our plans to start out for the sea."

Ernest began unwrapping the tissue-paper parcels none too happily. The little people seemed to him just a shade too pleased at getting their home back. He was beginning to think that the trip to the coast was further away now than ever before.

Outside the house, across the street, Harwell and Sarah Mincing watched as the removal men unloaded the last pieces of furniture.

"So it has been sold then?" said Harwell, unaware that the house had *not* been sold but that its previous owner had returned.

"And what difference does that make to you?" asked Sarah. "When your precious fairy folk have gone away— flown off, no doubt, on their gossamer fairy wings to pastures new," she scoffed.

Harwell bit back a sharp reply. There were times when it seemed best not to argue with his sister over the reality of the mannikins. "They have gone off, sister, in the boot-boy's blacking-box. That much we *do* know. But I would have liked another chance to examine those premises before the new tenants moved in."

"To what purpose?"

"To look for *clues*, Sarah! Something that the boot-black urchin might have left behind that would give us some hint as to where he's gone. How am I to follow him if I don't know where he's headed for?"

"Your days of trespassing in that residence are well and truly over, Harwell," sniffed Sarah. "I doubt that the new tenants, whoever they are, will be as gullible as the photographer was."

"You're right, sister," admitted Harwell, with a sigh. "I was glad to see the back of the old goat, but I have to agree that he did serve our purpose—" He broke off as he glanced over his shoulder along the street and reacted with horror. "Speak of the devil and his attendant brood. *Hide*, sister!" Harwell grabbed hold of his sister and roughly thrust her into a nearby shop doorway.

Millie, the housemaid, gave no more than a passing glance at the two black-garbed figures with their backs to her. She was returning from her trip to the local shops and was in a hurry to be home. Cook, she knew, was anxious to start preparing the master's dinner.

As the housemaid's footsteps receded along the street, the two Mincings turned in the shop doorway and watched her retreating back.

"Millie Lottersby!" gasped Sarah. "That slattern! The flibbertigibbet that wasted my black-leading as if she were a high-born lady spreading butter on a crumpet!"

"A fig for your black-leading, Sarah," snarled Harwell.

"But what's she doing back here?" said Sarah. "She went off to the country with the fool photographer."

"Precisely!" snapped Harwell. "And if she is back, we may safely assume, I fancy, that the old goat himself is back in town as well. He's returned to roost, confound him!"

"But *why*?"

"Why? Why! Is it not obvious why? Because he's learnt somehow of the existence of the little creatures that he's had concealed beneath his roof—that's *why*, sister! He's come back to town to hunt down what is rightly mine. No doubt he has some inkling of where the boot-black ragamuffin has taken them off to. He plans to steal them!" Harwell paused and his mouth twisted as he raised his hands, fingers outstretched. "Oh, if only I could slip these around the old fool's spindly throat this instant—I'd make him pay for it!" he snarled. "Meanwhile, I must needs infiltrate that dwelling-place one more time, Sarah—I must question the old goat closely."

"But he knows you, Harwell—present yourself before him and he will recognize you immediately."

A smile spread slowly across Harwell's face and he tapped the side of his nose with his forefinger in familiar fashion. "Have no fear, Sarah. He will not recognize me in the disguise that I have planned on this occasion."

"Not disguises again!" moaned Sarah. "Surely you've run the gamut of false moustaches and funny noses from beggar-man to thief! Why not, for once, knock on his door and confront him in your true light—that of a dedicated madman!"

"This shall be the very last time, sister, that I must needs take recourse to costume," replied Harwell, gruffly. "And the disguise that I have decided upon is foolproof."

"How many times have we heard *that* before?"

"You heard me mention earlier that I need to search that house for clues—I shall go there in a disguise which will suit that very purpose."

Sarah Mincing frowned. She wondered what fanciful scheme her brother had concocted this time? She peered into his face. But there was nothing in Harwell's expression that gave her a hint as to his intentions.

It was early evening and the removal men had left some hours before. The street was empty except for some urchins playing around a lamp-post and an oddly garbed figure standing outside the Garstanton front door.

The stranger was wearing a deer-stalker cap and a loud check overcoat which reached down to the ground. There was a large magnifying glass sticking out of one of the overcoat's pockets. The man had a hooked pipe clenched between his teeth and his face was framed by a bushy black beard. He reached up and banged loudly with the door knocker three times.

Inside the house, Ernest and the Lilliputians were back on the landing of the top floor. They were keeping a watch on the floors below, awaiting an opportunity when they might send the boy down after food. They looked at each other as they heard the knocking on the front door.

"Callers?" said Spelbush, suspiciously. "On the first day back in residence? Unusual, to say the least."

"Are you thinking what I'm thinking, Spelbush?" said Fistram.

"And me," said Brelca. "Harwell Mincing."

Spelbush nodded, gravely. "You stay here," he said to Ernest. "We'll go down and investigate."

The three Lilliputians set off lowering themselves down the stairs, at speed, in the manner which they had practised over the months.

Millie, meanwhile, had come up from the kitchen and now opened the front door. She blinked in surprise as she saw the oddly dressed man standing outside.

"Yessir?" she mumbled.

"Be so good as to inform your master," said Harwell Mincing, for sure enough it *was* him lurking behind the bushy beard, "that Sergeant Lashwood Pearce of the City's Force of Detectives would like a private word with him."

"Coo-er!" gasped Millie, impressed.

Minutes later, Harwell was being ushered up the stairs towards the parlour.

The three little people, hiding under the what-not on the first-floor landing, nudged each other as they watched Harwell's boots walk past. Cunning as Harwell was, he had never yet had the sense to change his footwear when in disguise. Consequently, the little people had been able to recognize him every time.

"In here, sir," said Millie, opening the parlour door.

"Come in, officer—good evening to you!" said Mr Garstanton, rising to greet his visitor.

"Good evening to you too, sir," replied Harwell.

Although the photographer had only moved back into his home that day, the carpets, curtains and furniture were all back in place and a cosy fire burned in the grate.

"Thank you, Millie. That will be all," said Mr Garstanton.

Millie bobbed a curtsy and went out, closing the door behind her. But the Lilliputians had already snatched at the opportunity and slipped into the room unnoticed. They were now concealed under the writing bureau by the door.

"And how can I be of service to the City's Detective Force?" asked Mr Garstanton, who had failed to see through Harwell's disguise.

"By giving me some information, I hope, sir," replied Harwell. "I am hot on the trail of a master criminal. An erstwhile boot-black who has forsworn that noble profession for a life of foul and heinous crime."

"Tut-tut-tut," said Mr Garstanton.

"Tut-tut indeed, sir," said Harwell. "Believe me, this green and pleasant land we live in will be a safer place by far when this particular black-hearted villain is put where he rightly belongs—behind prison bars picking oakum."

While this conversation was taking place, the three Lilliputians had made their way unobserved around the room, dodging under one piece of furniture after another, until they had taken up their position behind the coal scuttle.

Mr Garstanton stroked his chin. "I still don't understand where I fit into your enquiries, Sergeant?"

"Why, sir, because this very house presents the backdrop to one of the scoundrel's most audacious crimes."

"Is that a fact, Sergeant?"

"It is indeed, sir. He was known to break one of the downstairs windows here some nights ago and gain entry to the premises."

"And is he hiding in here somewhere now?" asked Mr Garstanton, glancing anxiously around the room.

"If only he was, sir!" said Harwell, with a shake of his head. "Why, I'd have the handcuffs on the rogue in an instant—and then you might all sleep easier in your beds. The villain has moved on—but it's not beyond the bounds of possibility that he might return—either to this house or to the neighbourhood."

"In which case, Sergeant, you may rest assured that I shall keep my eyes well peeled," said Mr Garstanton. "Do you have a description of the blaggard?"

"I do indeed, sir. Fair complexion, blue eyes and standing about so tall," said Harwell, indicating Ernest's height with one of his hands.

Mr Garstanton raised his eyebrows. "Good heavens!" he exclaimed. "Is he a dwarf?"

"Not exactly, sir. More in the nature of a scheming ragamuffin."

"Do you mean to say that he's a *boy*?"

Unnoticed by both Harwell and Mr Garstanton, the three Lilliputians had crept out stealthily from behind the coal scuttle. Carrying a stick of kindling wood apiece and hiding from sight behind Harwell's floor-length overcoat, they had crept into the centre of the fireplace in front of the blazing grate. Now, using the sticks of wood, they were poking burning embers out from underneath the fire and pushing them towards the hem of Harwell's coat.

"A *boy*, d'y'say?" repeated Mr Garstanton, unaware of what was going on behind Harwell's back. "And how old, pray, is this master criminal you're chasing?"

Harwell shrugged. "Ten or eleven or thereabouts. He carries with him a wooden boot-black box—about so deep and about so much across." As he spoke, Harwell described the box's dimensions with his hands. "It is this box in particular that I am anxious to lay my hands on. You have not seen either box or boy, I take it?"

"No, Sergeant, I have not!" said Mr Garstanton and his voice rose angrily as he continued. "And I must confess that I am not altogether sure that I would communicate the fact to you if I had! A boy indeed! Ten or eleven years old?"

The Lilliputians, having pushed the red-hot coals underneath the hem of Harwell's overcoat, were making their way back towards the coal scuttle.

"Ten or eleven or thereabouts," repeated Harwell, unaware that the hem of his overcoat was beginning to smoulder.

"And you can speak of putting a child of such tender years behind bars?" said Mr Garstanton, angrily.

"I can, sir! I do, sir! I would indeed, sir!" growled Harwell, not much liking the way the conversation seemed to be going. "Boy or no boy, if I could get my hands on the scoundrel, I'd make things very hot for him, believe you me—"

"Excuse me, Sergeant," broke in Mr Garstanton in some concern. He had noticed the spiral of smoke that was rising from Harwell's coat.

"Pray don't interrupt me, sir!" snapped Harwell. "As I was saying, I would make things very hot for him indeed— blazing hot, in fact!"

"Do forgive me, Sergeant, for butting in—but I do feel I ought to tell you that you seem to be on fire."

"Eh? What!" Harwell, who could now smell the smoke, glanced behind him and saw the flames that were now beginning to dance up around the bottom of his coat. "Ow! Ooooh! Aaaagh!" he cried, leaping from one foot to the other.

"The kitchen, Sergeant!" cried Mr Garstanton, throwing open the parlour door. "This way! *Quickly!*" Then moving out on to the landing himself, he leaned over the banister and called down into the hall. "Fire! *Fire!* Millie! All hands man the pumps! *Fire!*"

"YeeeaaAGGHH!" and "YeeeoOOOWWW!" yelled Harwell, prancing unhappily down the stairs with the smoke and flames billowing out behind him.

Harwell and Millie arrived in the hall at one and the same time but from opposite directions, Harwell with his overcoat on fire. Millie, having heard Mr Garstanton's cries, was carrying a bucket of cold water. The housemaid drew back her arms and then flung the contents of the bucket over Harwell.

WhoooOOOSSSHH!

"Well done, Millie," complimented Mr Garstanton. "That seems to have done the trick."

It had indeed. And not only had the water doused the flames, it had also drenched Harwell from head to foot. Harwell did not appear at all pleased. He stood in the hall, shivering from the cold, dripping water on to the floor and trying to hide the fact that his beard was coming adrift.

"This way, Sergeant," said Mr Garstanton, ushering the sodden figure along the hall.

"'E seemed a funny sort of policeman, if you arst me, sir," said Millie, after the front door had closed on Harwell. "Beggin' yer pardin, sir, but what was it 'e was wanting?"

"A boy, Millie," said Mr Garstanton, sorrowfully shaking his head. "Our gallant police force, or so it would seem, has massed its forces in pursuit of some unfortunate urchin boy."

"Well, I never!" said Millie as her employer set off sadly towards the parlour.

At the same time, proud at their victory over the enemy, the Lilliputians were well on their way back to the top landing. Once there, they would recount the tale of their brave deed, over and over again, to Ernest.

5

Later that same night, Mr Garstanton sat alone at the dining table. There were several bowls of vegetables on the table and a plate containing two grilled chump chops lay in front of him. But the food stood untouched and cold.

There was a tap on the door and Millie entered, carrying a tray. "Begging yer pardin, sir," she said, "I knows as 'ow you ain't rung down nor nothing, but seeing as 'ow it's after half past nine o'clock and Cook's corns is giving 'er gyp—what with the travelling back and that—is it all right for me to clear the table?"

"What?" said Mr Garstanton, who had been deep in thought. "Oh! By all means, Millie, clear away—clear away. I'd entirely forgotten the time."

Millie went to the table where she pulled up in surprise. "Why, bless my soul, sir!" she said. "But you ain't touched anything at all!"

"I'm afraid I've little appetite," said Mr Garstanton with a sigh. "It's been a long day—perhaps Cook's not alone in being affected by the travelling."

"I know what will tempt your fancy, sir," said Millie, loading the dishes on to the tray. "The apple pie and custard what's for afters."

"I'm afraid I'm going to decline the pudding course too," said Mr Garstanton with a shake of his head. "My apologies to Cook, Millie. Tell her I'm sure the apple pie is delicious and that I shall tackle it tomorrow."

"Yes, sir, very good, sir," said Millie, loading the dishes on to the dumb-waiter.

She tugged on the rope, sending the dumb-waiter down towards the kitchen. But the moment that she left the room, the dumb-waiter stopped and then began to move in the opposite direction. Mr Garstanton was sitting with his back to the hatch so he did not see that the dumb-waiter was now travelling upwards, heading towards the nursery.

"Hey up!" cried Ernest, who had pulled on the dumb-waiter's rope. "There's all sorts of stuff on here." He examined the contents of the dumb-waiter's shelves by the glow of a candle that he was holding.

"Sharply does it then, boy," said Spelbush.

The three little people were sitting round the dining table in the dolls' house, waiting to be served.

"It will go down again any second," said Brelca.

"What's on the menu?" asked Fistram.

" 'Ot taters?" said Ernest, picking food off the dishes with his free hand and putting it on a plate.

" 'Ot taters?" repeated Spelbush, not understanding.

"I think he means hot potatoes," said Brelca.

"Fascinating!" said Spelbush. " 'Ot taters, eh? I must write that down. We've been here all these months and we're only now beginning to hear the language. I wish he'd use more of his native tongue."

"I wish he'd get on with serving dinner," said Fistram.

"I'm being as quick as I can," said Ernest, picking off more vegetables. "There's carrots, there's cauliflower and there's chops as well —"

But even as he spoke, the dumb-waiter began to descend

again as someone tugged on the rope from down below.

"That's as much as I could get," said Ernest, going towards the dolls' house with the plate of food that he had managed to filch. "There was some gravy in a gravy-boat as well, but I couldn't pick it out with my fingers."

"It's *cold!*" complained Fistram as Ernest held the plate of food out towards him.

"It's not *my* fault," said Ernest.

Downstairs in the kitchen, Millie waited for the dumb-waiter to descend. "I could have sworn I sent it back down 'ere when I was in the dining room," she said to Cook. "But it somehow seems to 'ave gone up to the nursery."

"Seems to me," said Cook, who was giving her tired feet a mustard-bath in a bowl in front of the kitchen fire, "as if you don't know whether you're coming or going today, girl."

"I know," said Millie with a sigh. "I'm that there worried about the master being off his food—sitting up there—all by hisself—as lonely as a needle in an 'aystack, as the saying goes. He enn'arf missing 'is grandchildren, Cook, an' that's a fact!"

"I'm sure you're right, Millie—but there's nothing we can do about it," said Cook, reaching for the towel which was on the back of a chair. "As soon as I've dried me feet, I'm off to bed."

"Same here," said Millie, "as soon as I've unloaded this lot." The dumb-waiter had now arrived and she was lifting off the vegetable dishes. "That's funny!" she said.

"What's that?"

"I could have sworn that there was *two* chump chops on this plate when I sent it down—now there's only one. An' these 'ere vegetables seems to be less than what there was."

Cook shook her head. "It's like I say, Millie. It's been a long hard day for all of us. You're just imagining things."

"I suppose you're right," said Millie, sighing again.

Upstairs in the nursery, the Lilliputians had cleared their plates.

"What's for pudding?" asked Fistram.

"There isn't any," said Ernest.

"But we *always* have a pudding," said Fistram.

Ernest shrugged. "There was some apple pie or something on that lift thing—but it went back down again too quickly for me to grab any."

"I must say," said Brelca, hungrily, "that I wouldn't say 'no' to a slice of apple pie."

"Very well, we'll have apple pie," said Spelbush. "The boy will go down and bring some from the kitchen as soon as the servants are abed."

"No, he won't!" snapped Ernest.

"We have an arrangement, boy," said Spelbush, sharply. "You will provide our rations and, in return, we shall take you to the sea."

"So you keep saying, but we never seem to set off," Ernest pointed out.

"Patience, boy—we will, we will," said Spelbush. "You have my word on that. You carry out your part of the bargain and forage in the kitchen."

"But it will be dark down there," said Ernest, pointing at the candle-stub which was about to flicker out. "I'll probably trip over something and wake the whole house up."

"The boy's right," said Spelbush, turning to his companions. "*We* know that kitchen like the back of our hands— one of us must go with him."

"Yes. How about it, Fistram?" said Brelca, not wishing to investigate the kitchen in the dead of night.

"You're our leader, Spelbush," said Fistram, who didn't much fancy the trip either. "You go."

"It's because I *am* the leader that I must remain behind and stay in command of things," said Spelbush, who had little enthusiasm for the venture either.

"Huh," said Ernest, scornfully, "you're all afraid!"

But Spelbush, frightened as he was, would not admit it. "We are Lilliputians, lad," he said. "And Lilliputians do not know the meaning of fear. We'll prove it to you too—we'll all go." As he spoke, he glowered sternly at both Fistram and Brelca, daring them to argue with him.

About half an hour later, with the house in total darkness, Ernest tiptoed out of the nursery and headed for the stairs. In his hands he carefully carried his boot-black box which contained three little people. The lid of the box was open and the Lilliputians, acting as navigators, stood in the front of the box instructing Ernest where to put his feet.

"Left foot—right foot—two more steps to the landing—look out for the bureau on your left—feel for the banister rail on your right . . ."

In this way, they made their way successfully and without mishap into the hall. But here things began to go wrong. A small table, which did not belong there, had been left in the hall by the removal men. Mr Garstanton had intended to move the table to its rightful place but had not yet found opportunity to do so.

Ernest walked straight into it.

Crash! The sound seemed to echo right round the house.

Ernest stood stock-still. The Lilliputians ducked down inside the box and held their breath.

Then, just when it seemed safe to move on again, a door was flung open on the first-floor landing. Mr Garstanton appeared in night-shirt and night-cap, carrying an oil-lamp.

"Who's there?" he demanded, holding the lamp above his head. The oil-lamp cast a glowing circle of orange light down into the hall, revealing Ernest clutching his box. "Why, bless my soul, it's a boy!" gasped Mr Garstanton in some surprise. "The boy with the boot-black box!" he said, recalling all that he had been told earlier that evening.

"Don't come near me, mister," said Ernest. Holding the boot-black box close to his chest, he backed fearfully towards the front door.

"Don't be afraid, boy," said Mr Garstanton. "I don't mean to harm you."

"I've told you—stay where you are," warned Ernest, as the old photographer took a step across the landing towards the stairs.

"I only wish a word with you," pleaded Mr Garstanton. "Believe me, I'm not going to hand you over to the—"

But he never finished his sentence. Ernest turned suddenly and ran down the hall. The boy scrabbled with the bolts on the front door, the boot-box held awkwardly under one arm.

"Stay! Please, wait, I beg you!" cried Mr Garstanton, now hurrying down the stairs towards the boy.

It was a close thing, but Ernest just managed to unbolt the door, fling it open and run out into the night before the photographer reached him. Mr Garstanton stood at the open door in his night-shirt, the oil-lamp held aloft, listening to the boy's footsteps as Ernest was swallowed up in the darkness.

"What is it, sir? What's 'appening?" Millie, also in her

71

night-gown, had come out of her bedroom to find out what was going on.

"Nothing to alarm yourself about," explained Mr Garstanton. "It seems that we have had a visitor—a small boy carrying a boot-black box."

"The same one that copper was chasing?" asked the housemaid, coming down the stairs.

"I imagine so. I cannot conceive that there are two such similar boys wandering the streets at this hour."

Master and maid stood at the open door and peered out into the dark of night.

"I 'opes as 'ow 'e never catches the poor lad then," said Millie, adding, "Do you fink the little chap will be all right out there?"

"That, Millie, is something I'm afraid that we are not likely to discover," said Mr Garstanton, gravely. "Let us hope and pray so."

"I wonder what it is that he carried around in his boot-black's box?" pondered the housemaid.

Mr Garstanton shook his head and shrugged. "I don't suppose we shall ever know that either," he said, closing the door.

Outside, in the street, there was only silence.

The next morning dawned clear but frostily cold.

About a mile from the Garstanton house, in the poorest part of the town, a hard-faced, red-cheeked man stamped his feet and blew on his hands. The gold buttons on his uniform coat were fastened tightly over his fat stomach. His name was Silas Elmwood and he was the official in charge of the town's orphans and pauper children.

Elmwood was standing outside a pair of battered wooden

gates across which, in paint-peeling letters, was inscribed the legend:

EBENEEZER LOWTHWAITE

UNDERTAKER

CONTRACT FUNERALS FOR THE POOR

OUR SPECIALITY

"About time too!" growled Elmwood as the gates creaked slowly open.

They had been drawn apart by the undertaker's apprentice, a boy in ragged clothing. A moment later, a horse-drawn cart clattered out of the yard. The cart, which contained a cheaply fashioned plain wood coffin, was covered by a tarpaulin sheet stretched over three metal hoops.

The undertaker, Ebeneezer Lowthwaite, sat on the cart's driving-seat, whip in hand. He was dressed in a shabby black suit and wore a faded top-hat. He had a gloomy face and was as thin as the tired horse that struggled between the shafts of his cart.

A poorly dressed girl followed on foot behind the horse and cart. Her name was Emily Wilkins. She was just twelve years old and was the only mourner at her mother's funeral. Emily's face expressed her sorrow, but her cheeks were dry. She had cried all the tears that she had to shed some days before.

As this sad procession rattled off along the cobbled street, bound for the local cemetery, Silas Elmwood fell into step beside the cart on the pavement. It was his job to return Emily to the workhouse after the burial had been completed.

Emily Wilkins and Silas Elmwood were not to know that fate had other plans in store for her that day.

That same morning, after breakfast in the Garstanton home, Millie took down her employer's overcoat from the hall-stand and helped him to put it on.

"I 'opes as 'ow you're doing the right thing, sir, going out this morning," she said, as she brushed his coat all over with the stiff brush that was always kept on the hall-stand for that purpose. "It ain't 'alf chilly out today. I dunno but what you wouldn't be better off to let me fetch yer morning paper while you sits in front of the parlour fire with your feet up."

"Nonsense, Millie! Don't pamper me. The fresh air will do me the world of good. I might even take a turn round the park lake while I'm out."

"P'raps you're right, sir," said the housemaid. "Why don't you do that, eh? It'd give you an appetite for lunch."

"Speaking of lunch, sir," said Cook, popping her head round the kitchen door, "I wonder if I might beg a word with you afore you goes out?"

"As many of 'em as you wish, Cook, ask away!" said Mr Garstanton.

"I'm wondering what I might tempt you with today, sir? You being so hard to please of late. How would it be if I were to ask the butcher to let me have a nice leg of pork?"

"A good idea, Cook," said Mr Garstanton, heading for the door. "I'm sure that both you and Millie will enjoy it—though I don't imagine that I shall require any more

74

than a piece of cheese. I'll see you both anon . . ." With which, he went out into the street.

The door closed behind him.

Millie shook her head and sighed. "'E ain't eating nothing!" she said to Cook. "An' 'e ain't looking none too good in 'isself neither. 'E ain't 'ad the appetite of a sparrow, so 'e ain't, not since 'is grandchildren left. An' you mark my words, Cook, 'e *won't* perk up neither—not till 'e finds something fresh to take 'is interest."

"Well, it won't be that Cheddar cheese that you fetched in yesterday, Millie—because that wasn't fresh a week ago. I can hardly give that to the master for his lunch. I can't imagine why you let the grocer palm it off on you!" And so saying, Cook headed back towards the kitchen.

Millie shrugged her shoulders apologetically, and scuttled off about her household tasks.

As it happened, Mr Garstanton was not the only person bound for the park that morning. Harwell and Sarah Mincing had set out for the very same place some time before. They were, in fact, approaching the park's huge wrought-iron front gates at that very moment.

"Remove your hat, brother," ordered Sarah, digging Harwell in the ribs and drawing his attention to the horse-drawn hearse that was moving slowly along the road in their direction. "Show a little respect, if you please, for someone who will reach the Kingdom of Heaven before you."

Harwell stopped, took off his bowler hat and lowered his eyes towards the gutter as the cart containing the coffin rattled along the road.

As the cart drew level with them, Sarah took note of the solitary girl walking behind. She also recognized the children's officer who strolled alongside.

"That's sufficient, Harwell," sniffed Sarah, as the small procession moved past. "It's no more than a pauper's funeral. Another poverty-stricken wretch going off to meet its Maker and leaving a child behind as a burden on the parish," she snapped. "Is it not uncivil enough of the poor to *live* beyond their means—they must also *die* in the same uncaring manner?"

"Amen to that, sister," said Harwell, replacing his black bowler on his head.

The two Mincings continued on their way into the park as the funeral cart with its solitary mourner went on towards the cemetery.

6

"Paper! *Paper!* Read-all-abaht-it!" called the news-paper-seller who had set up his pitch close by the large imposing statue of a past town alderman in the centre of the park. "Latest news on the Boxer Uprising! All the very latest news from China! British troops in gallant stand! Paper, paper! *Read all abaht it!*"

"I'll take one of those, boy," said Harwell Mincing. The newspaper-seller handed Harwell a paper and received a penny in return. "I also seek some information," Harwell whispered into the news-boy's ear.

Sarah Mincing, sitting on the bench some yards away, watched her brother disapprovingly before turning her attention to the Bible she had taken out of her handbag.

Harwell strolled across, sat down beside her and opened his paper.

"It has not escaped my notice, brother, that you still have pennies to fritter away on newspapers—despite your constant claims of being hard-pressed for funds," observed Sarah, coldly. "I trust it was not the self-same penny that I handed to you in church for the collection last Sunday?"

Harwell cleared his throat and shuffled uneasily on his seat. "Not at all, Sarah," he stammered. "I happened to find a coin in the lining of my jacket. I purchased the newspaper in order to keep myself informed of the political situation in China."

"Informed of the horse-racing situation more likely," snapped his sister.

"How's that, Sarah?" asked Harwell, nervously.

"I'm sure that a study of those pages, Harwell, would confirm my belief that they contain the details of this afternoon's horse-race meetings."

"I wouldn't know about that, sister," said Harwell, swiftly turning over the page that he had been studying and which did indeed show particulars of the day's race-meetings. "If you must know, Sarah, the *real* reason that I bought the paper was in order to engage the news-boy in conversation."

"Indeed? And what might you hope to learn of benefit from a ragamuffin news-lad?"

"The location, perhaps, of a ragamuffin boot-black urchin," said Harwell, tapping the side of his nose with his forefinger in his usual manner. "Child-labourers, I've found, are frequently aware of each other's whereabouts."

Sarah sniffed, disbelievingly. "And *had* he seen the ragamuffin that we're looking for?"

"No—"

"I thought as much."

"But he knew of someone who had, sister! The hot-potato man who stands outside the gates of the park, Sarah, had told him of a boot-black boy who purchased *two* hot potatoes not an hour ago!"

"And what proof do you have that it's the same boot-black boy that we are looking for?" demanded Sarah. "Do you imagine, brother, that there is but one boot-black wretch in this town?"

"No, sister," replied Harwell, knowingly. "But I do believe that there is but one boot-black who needs *two* hot potatoes: one for himself, the other to feed the little creatures he keeps concealed within his boot-black box."

"Nonsense!"

"It's *true*, Sarah! Believe me! They cannot be far from where we sit at this very minute! We have the word of the news-boy ragamuffin who had it straight from the lips of the hot-potato man!"

Sarah snapped shut her Bible angrily. "News-boy ragamuffins!" she stormed. "Boot-black urchins! Hot-potato hawkers! Are these the company that we are now obliged to keep? Why, when Mother was alive, God rest her soul, she would not so much as deign to speak even to the green-grocer except that it be through the house-keeper. News-boys! Boot-blacks! Potato-men! If this farrago continues longer, you'll have me sitting down to tea with the chimney-sweep!"

"Aye, and I would do that too, sister," snarled Harwell, "if I thought that such a meeting would gain us more information regarding the little sly-booted creatures."

"Information!" sneered Sarah. "A fig for your information, Harwell! I suppose you threw more good money after bad and paid for the information that came at second-hand from the hot-potato man via the newspaper-lad?"

"Only another penny, Sarah," mumbled Harwell.

"*Another* penny? And I suppose you found that one too in the lining of your pocket? Or did you steal it from my purse?" said Sarah, bitterly. "Pennies for papers; pennies for information; pennies for this; pennies for that—a fool and his pennies are soon parted, Harwell Mincing! And all in pursuit of worthless—"

"Look out!" Harwell broke in, warningly. Sarah followed her brother's glance. Mr Garstanton was strolling along the path in their direction. Acting quickly, Sarah opened her Bible and held it up, hiding her face. Harwell, meanwhile, had hidden himself behind the open pages of his newspaper.

Not that they need have worried.

The old photographer was far too absorbed in his own thoughts to notice them. He was wondering about his grandchildren and hoping that they were enjoying themselves at that moment.

Harwell, however, had decided that Mr Garstanton's thoughts were following a similar path to his own. "What did I say, sister?" he snapped at Sarah as the old photographer ambled past. "Did I not tell you that the little folk were hereabouts—the jackals are gathering already!"

Sarah was not listening. She was looking, horrified, at the Bible she had been holding up in front of her face. "What am I doing?" she said, aghast. "Hiding behind the Holy Bible? Using God's book to facilitate the Devil's work!"

"I always said that the old goat knows more about this business than he cares to pretend," growled Harwell, ignoring his sister's words. "Is it possible, do you think, that the old fool knows where to lay hands on the mannikins?"

"I only wonder, brother, to what depths of depravity you will drag me down next," said Sarah, still pursuing her own train of thought.

"I'll follow the old goat, Sarah," said Harwell, folding up his newspaper and tucking it under one arm. "If I'm not back within the hour, make your way to our chambers and

I'll join you there. I don't suppose, in the event that I'm required to take a hansom-cab, you'd care to subsidize the venture?"

But Sarah was still concerned about the twopence squandered already that morning on the news-boy. By the look on his sister's face, Harwell could see she was not going to give him a single penny-piece out of her purse.

"Forget what I said, sister," Harwell concluded sadly and, getting to his feet, he set off to follow Mr Garstanton through the park.

"And how long, boy, do you intend that we should remain cooped up in this hovel?" demanded Spelbush, looking round at the dingy wooden walls.

The three Lilliputians and Ernest were sitting on the floor of a draughty wooden hut that they had come across in the middle of the previous night. There were shovels and rakes and other rusting gardening tools propped up in a corner of the shed. Ernest was gnawing at the remains of a baked potato. The little people were sitting on upturned plant-pots, using a larger upturned plant-pot as a table and sharing the second baked potato between them. It had, of course, been Ernest who, in the dark of early morning, had gone out and brought back the baked potatoes from the hot-potato man.

Ernest shrugged in answer to Spelbush's question. "We could stay in here until it's dark again," he said, "and then move on tonight."

"Stay *here*?" wailed Fistram. "Until it's *night*?"

"Why not?" asked Ernest.

"Because it's draughty and it's uncomfortable," moaned Fistram. "And besides, it'll be hours and hours before it's dark again—it's only morning now."

"I'm not staying in here when it gets dark again," announced Brelca. "It was horrible last night. I'm sure an enormous spider walked across me—and back again."

"Spiders can't hurt you!" jeered Ernest. "You're not scared of a titchy little spider, surely?"

"Not a titchy *little* spider, no," said Brelca, sharply. "Not a *my* size spider. But a *your* size spider—a great, ginormous spider—a *giant's* spider—if you want the truth, I *am* afraid, yes."

"And what about *food*?" put in Fistram. "You're not suggesting we're to survive all day on a single baked potato, surely?"

Ernest sighed. He could have reminded Fistram of the time when he had suggested that a single radish might provide a meal for all four of them. But what was the use of arguing?

"Don't ask me what we're going to eat," said the boy at last. "These hot spuds cost me the last twopence I had in all the world. I don't know where our next meal is coming from."

"Take heart, boy," said Spelbush, leaping down from his plant-pot. "Leave that problem to me on this occasion. You concentrate on conveying us around in that box of yours. I shall take on the provision of rations—as leader of this expedition."

"Bravo, Spelbush!" cried Brelca. "It takes a Lilliputian to tackle a difficult problem."

"Tell the boy how you intend to feed us, Spelbush," said Fistram.

"Simplicity itself," said Spelbush, airily. "I use my eyes, you see—and what my eyes behold is then transferred to my brain—the brain takes in all the facts and moves into action like a well-oiled steam-engine—click, click—whirr, whirr—problem solved!"

"Well *done*, Spelbush!" said Brelca, clapping her hands.

"Not at all," replied Spelbush, preening the end of his beard between forefinger and thumb. "Some things come easily to me."

"Stop boasting, Spelbush," said Fistram. "How *do* you propose to feed us?"

Spelbush shook his head, pityingly, at Fistram's inability to see what was plainly in front of his face. "Where have we just spent the night?" he asked.

"Why—here of course," said Fistram, puzzled.

"And where is 'here'?"

"In this hut," replied Fistram. "And a more uncomfortable place I've seldom had to put up with! But what has that got to do with food?"

"What *kind* of a hut is it?" asked Spelbush, patiently.

"A *garden* hut, of course," said Fistram, nodding at the spades and other garden implements.

"Precisely! A *garden* hut! So—my eyes tell me that we're in a garden hut. My brain assimilates the facts. Click, click—snap, snap and *whirr*! Outside that door, says brain, there lies a garden!"

"Well?" said Fistram.

"What grows in a garden, Fistram?"

"Flowers," said Fistram.

"Plants," said Brelca.

"Where would you two be without me?" said Spelbush, shaking his head in despair. "*Vegetables*, of course! Lettuces, tomatoes, carrots, etcetera, etcetera! A veritable vegetarian feast!"

"You are a wise old stick, Spelbush," said Brelca, admiringly.

"And not only vegetables," Spelbush continued. "But also fruit: raspberries; gooseberries; blackcurrants—why, all we need to do is to push open that door and we shall feast our eyes upon a banquet!"

"You won't, you know."

It was Ernest who had spoken.

"Did you say something, boy?" said Spelbush.

Ernest nodded, solemnly. "I said, 'you won't, you know'—feast your eyes on a banquet. If you don't believe me, go and look—there's a crack in the bottom of that wall. Over there."

Spelbush went to the wall and peered through the crack between the boards. "The boy's right," he said in hollow tones. "It isn't a garden after all—it's a graveyard."

"A graveyard?" squeaked Fistram.

"A graveyard," repeated Spelbush.

"This isn't a gardener's hut, either," said Ernest. "It's a gravedigger's shed."

"Good old Spelbush," said Brelca sarcastically, "wherever would we be without him?"

"I know exactly where we are *with* him," said Fistram. "In a gravedigger's shed."

"That's hardly my fault! I didn't bring us here—*he* did!" Spelbush glowered at Ernest, then, glancing at the boot-black box, he added, "In that thing. What a way to travel. In a boot-black box!"

"What a place to end up in," said Fistram, gloomily. "A gravedigger's shed."

"What did I say? Don't tell me that I didn't warn you!" said Brelca, stamping her foot in anger. "I said all along that we would be wrong to throw in our lot with another child!"

"At least you three were *dry* last night," said Ernest. "It was pouring down with rain. You were in the box. I had to look for somewhere to shelter. This was the only place that I could find." Again it occurred to him that he had had just about enough of the ungrateful Lilliputians. "If you're not satisfied, you can make your own way to the sea—and see if I care! It's only about fifty million trillion miles from here!"

The little people looked at each other in concern.

"Let us not act hastily, boy," said Spelbush. "Let's not any of us say something that we might later regret. We struck a bargain with you—we'll not go back on our word."

"Look outside again, Spelbush," said Fistram, quickly changing the subject. "What can you see beyond the graveyard?"

Spelbush glanced through the crack again. "I can't see beyond the graveyard. But something seems to be going on over there."

Ernest went to the door, opened it slightly and followed Spelbush's glance. "It's a funeral," he said.

The Lilliputians joined him at the foot of the door and peered out.

A short procession was moving along an avenue in the cemetery. It was led by a priest walking in front of a horse-drawn cart. The man on the driving-seat of the cart was thin and dressed all in black. He had a battered top-hat perched on his head. Another man walked beside the cart. He was very fat and wore the uniform of a town official. A poorly dressed girl was trudging along behind the cart.

The girl, of course, was Emily Wilkins.

85

The procession was making its way towards a spot where two men holding spades stood beside an open grave.

"It can't be a very important funeral," observed Spelbush. "It isn't a very grand procession."

"It isn't a bit important," said Ernest. "It's a contract funeral. A pauper's funeral."

"He looks quite important though," said Fistram. "The fat man with the gold buttons."

"Him?" said Ernest. "That's Silas Elmwood."

"You know him then?" asked Spelbush.

"There isn't a kid in this town that doesn't know him—and goes afeared of him," said Ernest. "He's the children's officer. He'll be there to take that lass to the workhouse after the funeral's over."

"The *workhouse*?" said Fistram.

"That poor little girl?" said Brelca.

"Tell me, boy," said Spelbush, "is it her desire to be taken to this workhouse?"

"*Desire!*" snorted Ernest. "Nobody *wants* to go to the workhouse. I've told you, he's the children's officer. He's *taking* her there—he'll drag her there if he has to."

The three Lilliputians looked at each other and frowned.

"Then someone ought to intervene and rescue that poor child," said Spelbush.

"Somebody ought to, yes," said Fistram.

"Indeed they should," said Brelca.

"It's all right saying *somebody*—but who?" asked Ernest.

But the Lilliputians had already made up their minds.

Across the cemetery, the horse and cart and its attendants had arrived at the place where the two gravediggers leant on their spades. It was a forlorn, drab area reserved only for the graves of paupers. There were no headstones to

86

be seen; only small hummocks of earth marked the places where the poor people of the town were buried.

"Whoa there!" cried the undertaker, Ebeneezer Lowthwaite, reining in his horse.

The two gravediggers put down their spades and moved to lift the coffin off the back of the cart. The priest walked to the open grave and opened his prayer book.

"Over there, lass—and be sharp about it!" snarled Silas Elmwood, pushing Emily roughly towards the graveside. "We don't want to hang about here any longer than is necessary."

The priest cleared his throat in readiness to begin the burial service.

Back in the gravediggers' hut, the Lilliputians were planning Emily's rescue.

"Are you all clear on what you have to do?" asked Spelbush who, it must be said, could be quite purposeful when the occasion demanded it.

Fistram, Brelca and Ernest all nodded to show that each knew the part they had to play.

"Good," said Spelbush. "And are you also sure, boy, that you can carry the three of us inside that box and manage the ball of twine and the garden rake as well?"

"Easy!"

"Off we go then," said Spelbush, climbing into the open boot-black box and beckoning his two companions to follow.

Once all three Lilliputians were safely in the box, Ernest closed the lid. Then, picking up the box, the ball of twine and the garden rake, he crept out of the shed.

Keeping his head low and dodging from behind one headstone to the next, Ernest set off across the cemetery towards the funeral which was about to take place.

While Ernest and the little people had been plotting the rescue of Emily Wilkins, Harwell Mincing had been dogging the old photographer's footsteps through the park and out of it.

Mr Garstanton's walk led him, naturally enough, back to his own home.

Harwell, having followed him all the way, ducked into his usual shop-doorway observation-post on the opposite side of the street. He watched the front door close behind his adversary. Harwell gnawed at his lower lip with frustration. He had tracked the old goat of a photographer for a good hour and more with nothing to show for it except a waste of shoe-leather. He turned in disgust to walk away and then jumped with fright as he realized that someone was standing close by his shoulder.

It was only Sarah.

"You startled me, sister," grumbled Harwell. "I thought we agreed to meet back at our chambers?"

"And what would have been the point of my going home, when I knew full well that I would find you here?" said Sarah with a sniff. "Wasting your time, as usual. And how did you enjoy your game of Hide-and-Seek with that dolt Garstanton?"

"Not at all," growled Harwell. "The crafty old goat led me thrice around the duck-pond in the park and then back here—a complete wild-goose chase."

"Don't talk to me of a wild-goose chase, Harwell—not after the madcap idiotic jaunt you've dragged me on all these months!"

From the very moment they had set out to capture the

little people, Sarah Mincing had been losing her enthusiasm for the chase.

The story had begun in Sarah's seaside boarding-house almost a year before. Mr Garstanton had been holidaying with his grandchildren. They had been staying at Miss Mincing's house when the children discovered the three shipwrecked Lilliputians on the beach. Harwell had been staying with his sister at the time. By chance, he had learnt of the existence of the Lilliputians—but just too late for him to do anything about it. The Garstantons had set off for home that morning.

Sarah, at her brother's insistence and on his promise of untold wealth, had closed down her boarding-house in order to accompany Harwell in his quest. They had been on the trail of the little people ever since. But Sarah Mincing had begun to despair. She felt that they would never catch the mannikins. Indeed, she often doubted their very existence—wondering if they lived only in her brother's imagination.

"Sarah, will you never accept proof positive—not even when it's presented to you before your very eyes? The little creatures *are* real, Sarah. Why else would that cunning conniving old fool of a photographer lead me on such a dance around the duck-pond, if not to throw me off the boot-black urchin's scent?"

"It would not occur to you, I suppose," suggested Sarah, "that Garstanton walked three times round the duck-pond today for no more sinister reason than to take the air?"

"Impossible, sister! I tell you, both the old goat and I are chasing the same pot of gold."

"And I myself, brother, am intent only on retaining my sanity!" retorted Sarah. "I tell *you*, Harwell, that if you

89

don't see sense and give up this foolish venture before the week is out, then I shall wash my hands of you entirely! It was bad enough when your fevered mind had got you pursuing your mythical fairy folk alone—but mythical fairy folk concealed in mythical boot-boy urchins' mythical boot-black boxes is stretching my good nature just that little bit too far!"

And so saying, Sarah Mincing turned on her heel and flounced off.

"Wait, Sarah!" pleaded Harwell, scurrying along at his sister's side. "The mannikins *do* exist, I promise you! The boot-black ragamuffin is real as well! You met him yourself, remember—you bade me give him twopence out of my own pocket. All we must do, Sarah, is find that brat and our fortunes are made . . . Bear with me, sister . . . for one more week . . ." Harwell huffed and puffed and panted as he struggled to keep up with his sister's pace and convince her at the same time. ". . . One more week, sister . . . and I swear to you that the brat, the box and the cunning creatures themselves shall all be mine."

But Sarah, ignoring all Harwell's entreaties, strode on firmly along the street.

7

". . . We meekly beseech thee, O Father," said the priest, standing by the grave into which the coffin had been lowered, "to raise us from the death of sin unto the life of righteousness . . ."

Emily Wilkins stood on the other side of the grave, head bowed and eyes closed. The two gravediggers waited some yards away, ready to finish their task. Beyond the gravediggers were Ebeneezer Lowthwaite and Silas Elmwood, leaning against the cart, paying no attention to the burial service and joking with each other.

But unbeknown to any of these, there were hidden watchers at the funeral. Ernest and Brelca were some twenty yards away behind the nearest headstone, waiting to put their plan into action. "How are Spelbush and Fistram doing?" asked Brelca. Ernest peered round the side of the headstone towards the horse and cart. He could just see the two Lilliputians hard at work behind one of the cart-wheels.

"They're getting on all right," whispered Ernest. "Do you know what you've got to do?"

Brelca nodded. "What about the rake?" she asked.

"I've put it where we said," whispered Ernest. "I think it's time to make a start. Off you go!"

Ernest, keeping his head down, watched from behind the

headstone as Brelca set off towards where the priest was still intoning the words from his prayer book over the grave. She managed easily to keep out of sight by dodging behind the long tufts of untended grass. Once Brelca was on her way, Ernest turned his attention to what was happening underneath the cart. Spelbush and Fistram were attaching a long length of twine to a spoke on one of the cart-wheels. It was no simple task, for to the Lilliputians the gardener's twine was like thick rope and difficult to handle.

Elmwood and Lowthwaite were totally unaware of the two small figures hard at work close to their feet. Silas Elmwood took a silver snuff-box out of his waistcoat pocket, flicked it open with his thumb and offered the contents to the undertaker.

"I'm much obliged to you, Mr Elmwood," said Ebeneezer Lowthwaite.

". . . and receive that blessing, which thy well-beloved Son shall then pronounce to all that love and fear thee," the priest's voice droned on as the burial service continued. "Come, ye blessed children of thy Father, receive the kingdom prepared for you from the beginning of the world . . ."

And all the while Emily Wilkins stood, eyes closed, head bowed, solemn-faced and lonely, with no idea that a plan to rescue her was already set in motion.

Ebeneezer Lowthwaite sniffed hard, twice, at the pinch of snuff on the back of his hand, drawing up the brown powder into each of his nostrils. He sneezed, spat, and then rubbed the spittle into the ground with the toe of his boot. He did this without bothering to glance down, which was lucky for the Lilliputians. Had the undertaker chosen to look towards his feet at that particular moment, he would have seen Spelbush Frelock tying a length of gardener's twine round his ankle.

And while Spelbush was fastening one end of the twine to Lowthwaite, Fistram was tying the other end round Elmwood's ankle. It was, of course, the same length of twine that was fastened to the cart-wheel spoke.

". . . The grace of our Lord Jesus Christ, and the love of God, and the fellowship of the Holy Ghost, be with us all evermore," intoned the priest, bringing the burial service to an end.

"Amen," said Emily Wilkins, softly.

The priest closed his prayer book and moved away, leaving the young girl alone with her thoughts at her mother's graveside.

Except that Emily was not entirely alone.

"Little girl!" said a small voice at her feet. "Little *girl!*"

Emily opened her eyes and was astonished to see a tiny person, not much higher than her ankle, looking up at her. Emily's mouth dropped open in surprise.

"Don't speak," said Brelca. "Listen to me carefully and then nod or shake your head. Do you understand?"

Emily Wilkins nodded.

"Is it your wish to be taken to the workhouse?" asked Brelca.

Emily Wilkins shook her head, fiercely.

"Then when you hear a boy call out to you to run—run towards him at once. And then do everything he tells you. Is that clear?"

Emily nodded again.

Having got the girl's assurance, Brelca scrambled up the hill of loose earth which was to be shovelled back into the grave. Once at the top, Brelca raised her arm above her head and waved towards the cart.

Fistram and Spelbush, now underneath the cart again, waved back to let her know they had completed their task.

Brelca turned and this time signalled to Ernest, hidden behind the headstone. All was ready.

Over by the cart, Silas Elmwood slipped his snuff-box back into his pocket. He took out a handkerchief, blew his nose loudly, and stretched himself. "Well then," he said to Lowthwaite, gruffly, "the workhouse waits for neither man nor child—she's had enough time I reckons to pay her last respects . . ."

It was at this moment exactly that Ernest's head bobbed up from behind the headstone. "Run, lass!" he called to Emily. "*Run!* Over here!"

Emily, requiring no second bidding, ran towards Ernest as fast as she was able.

"Hey, you!" snarled Elmwood. "You come back here, miss, or else you'll—"

But the children's officer never finished what he had started to say. For, as he spoke, he put out a foot to set off after Emily and was pulled up short by the stout twine around his ankle.

"AaaggGGHHH!" cried Elmwood, as he went crashing to the ground.

At the same time the twine jerked tight round the undertaker's foot, and Ebeneezer Lowthwaite came tumbling down on top of Silas Elmwood. The two men lay sprawling on the ground.

"What the hummers—" spluttered Elmwood.

"What the heckers—" stuttered Lowthwaite.

As the two men struggled to get to their feet, Ernest

Henshaw beckoned urgently to the girl as she ran towards him.

"This way!" cried the boy, setting off at full speed along one of the cemetery avenues. "And keep your head down!"

The Lilliputians were also running across the paupers' burial ground, but they went unnoticed by the children's officer, whose immediate concern was Emily.

"Don't stand there grinning like a pair of jackanapes!" he thundered at the two gravediggers as he struggled to free himself from Lowthwaite, adding, "And grab that lad as well! He's to blame for this, I'll warrant!"

The gravediggers, however, were too amused by the antics of the two men struggling with the bonds that held them to each other, to bother about the fleeing girl and boy.

Elmwood finally managed to free himself. But when he got to his feet there was no sign of either Emily or Ernest. "Where are you, lass!" he shouted, angrily. "You can't have got far, I know! Show yourself, Wilkins, or you'll suffer the worse for it when I do lay hold of you!"

But there was neither sight nor sound of the workhouse runaway.

Emily stood, hands on hips, slowly regaining her breath.

"Wait for me," said Ernest, who had led her safely back to the gravediggers' shed. "You'll be all right here for the minute."

Emily nodded. Then, as Ernest moved away, she frowned as she remembered something. "Hey, wait on!" she exclaimed. "Was I dreaming, or did I *really* see a little woman no bigger than that?" She put out her two forefingers and measured a distance of some twenty centimetres.

Ernest grinned. "Aye, there was," he said. "And there's

95

two little men the same size as her as well. It was them that tied up Elmwood and the undertaker. I've got to go and fetch them back. And put paid to Silas Elmwood."

The boy slipped out of the shed, closing the door behind him. Emily sank to the floor and pondered over what she had seen.

Back at the paupers' burial ground, Lowthwaite had also succeeded in standing up and was dusting down his funeral jacket and trousers with his hands. At the same time, he was glancing nervously around the cemetery.

"Give me a hand to search this graveyard, Mr Lowthwaite," said Elmwood. "She can't have got that far—no, nor the young hooligan that helped her neither."

"N-n-n-n-not me," stammered the undertaker. "I'm off! I reckon this place must be haunted!"

"Rubbish, man," growled Elmwood.

"Then who was it, if you please, that tied up my feet when there worn't no human person came within yards of me?" asked the undertaker with a shudder. "I tell you, I'm getting out of this—and the sooner the better!" And before Elmwood could make a move to stop him, Ebeneezer Lowthwaite had scrambled up on to the driving-seat of his cart and cracked the whip.

"Gee-up!"

The horse and cart rumbled off along the avenue towards the tall cemetery gates in a cloud of dust.

Silas Elmwood swung round on the two gravediggers. "What about you two fellows?" he said. "There's twopence apiece for you if the girl is caught—and sixpence to share if you fetch me back that lad as well."

"Nay, not me, master," said the first gravedigger. "I'll not lend a hand to put nobody in the workhouse."

"Nor me neither," agreed his workmate. "My job's gravedigging. It's not much, I'll grant you, but it's honest toil at least—and better than catching little children for a living."

The two men began shovelling the loose earth back into the open grave.

"Bad luck attend the both of you then," snarled Elmwood. "I'll find the lass myself!"

Some twenty yards away, Ernest and the Lilliputians were watching from behind a granite tomb with a carved angel on the top, its wings outspread. It was here that the four had agreed to meet. It was here too that the boy had left his boot-black box and the gardener's rake.

He now set the rake carefully along the path and then gestured at the box which stood open on the ground.

"Jump in," he whispered.

The little people scrambled quickly into the box, for they could already hear the approaching footsteps of the children's officer.

"Curse you, girl!" Elmwood muttered to himself as he peered this way and that. "I swear I'll thrash you within an inch of your life when I do find you!"

At this moment, Ernest's head appeared round the side of the granite tomb not far from where Elmwood stood. "Over here, Mister Elmwood!" the boy cried out in a cheeky voice.

"You young ruffian!" Elmwood shouted, waving his fist in anger. "I'll skin you alive, my lad!" And he took off in pursuit of Ernest at a lumbering run.

But the fat frame of the children's officer was no match in speed for the swift legs of the young boy. Ernest Henshaw had grown up in the rough-and-tumble of backstreet life.

He had been chased to no avail by far fitter men than Silas Elmwood. Ernest led the children's officer on a lively race round the cemetery, finally drawing him back to the avenue where he had set his trap.

The boy darted round a headstone, leapt lightly over the garden rake and barely paused in his stride to snatch up the boot-black box from the spot where he had left it.

Silas Elmwood, ten paces behind, turned the self-same headstone and his leading foot came down, heavily, on the rake's head.

The handle shot up swiftly and struck him full in the face.

"Thwack!"

The children's officer fell to the ground like a sack of potatoes. He lay there, moaning softly and feeling gingerly at his forehead.

Ernest did not stay to watch.

Moments later, the boy slipped back into the gravediggers' hut where Emily stood waiting. He put the boot-black box on a bench, then turned back to peer through the partly open door. Across the cemetery, he could see Silas Elmwood who had struggled to his feet and was wandering, groggily, around the headstones.

"He's going off," Ernest said to the girl. "But I reckon he'll be back again soon enough—we mustn't stay here much longer."

"What happened to them little people?" asked Emily.

Ernest nodded at the box.

Emily tiptoed over and gently lifted the lid.

Spelbush, Brelca and Fistram looked up into her face.

Emily gasped in amazement. "Aren't they strange?" she gasped. "They're a bit like dolls only . . . only real."

"Dolls! Dolls?" cried Brelca, angrily.

"There's gratitude for you!" said Spelbush. "I would have you know, little girl, that *I* am Spelbush Frelock—adventurer, explorer and proud Lilliputian. I did not instigate and organize your entire rescue single-handed just to be compared to a child's plaything!"

"Entire! Did you say *entire* rescue, Spelbush?" squealed Fistram. "I suppose my own involvement in the rescue was so insignificant as to be unnecessary?"

"I suppose that I need not have been there at all?" snapped Brelca.

"Nothing of the kind," said Spelbush. "All I said was that I was the one who instigated and organized the event. I wouldn't want to take any of the credit away from either of you. You were a great help. I could hardly have managed without you. I was only saying that the whole thing was *my* idea, that's all."

"Thanks very much!" said Brelca, tossing her head.

"For nothing!" added Fistram.

"Do they always argue with each other?" asked Emily, turning to Ernest.

Ernest grinned. "Most of the time they do," he said. "And when they're not quarrelling among themselves—they're usually taking it out on me."

Emily stared down into the boot-black box again. "They are teeny, aren't they?" she said. "But they are *bonny*!"

Spelbush almost turned blue in the face. His cheeks puffed out as if he were going to explode.

"They're a secret though," said Ernest, hastily. "You must never tell anybody that you've seen them."

"Oh, I won't, I won't!"

"Then swear it, faithfully," said Ernest.

"I, Emily Wilkins, being of sound mind and body —
that's what you're supposed to say when you swear anything," she explained to the little people, and then went on,
"—do swear on the grave of my poor mother that I shall
always keep this secret."

Ernest exchanged a meaningful glance with the Lilliputians. "Was it your mother's funeral then?" he asked
Emily.

Emily gave a solemn nod. "She'd been ill for ages. The
workhouse doctor said it was a blessing, her being took at
last." She paused and then added, fiercely, "She's better
off in heaven than in the workhouse—and they won't never
get me back in there neither!"

"We're running away as well," said Ernest.

"Excuse me, little boy," said Spelbush, clambering out
of the boot-black box. "*You* may be running away—*we* are
not engaged in any kind of a retreat."

"We're *advancing* to the coast," said Fistram, joining
Spelbush on the bench-top.

"We're taking this boy along with us," added Brelca.

"We're off to have a look at the sea," said Ernest.

"The sea!" gasped Emily. "I've never seen the sea."

"Neither have I," said Ernest.

"I wish I could come with you," said Emily, wistfully.

"You can if you want," said Ernest. "Why don't you?"

"Just a minute, boy, just a minute!" Spelbush broke in.
"That's quite out of the question."

"It's not up to you, boy, to take that sort of decision,"
said Fistram.

"We can't take any more children on board," said
Brelca. "One small boy is more than enough."

"We've saved you from the workhouse, little girl," said

Spelbush. "Be thankful for that—but now you are on your own."

Emily's shoulders drooped and she stared dolefully at her feet.

"You can't just *leave* her here!" said Ernest. "I don't call that much of a rescue."

The three Lilliputians looked at the downcast Emily and then at each other.

"I suppose two children could forage twice as much food as one," proffered Fistram.

"And she could take her turn at carrying us in the box," said Spelbush. "That way we would travel all the faster."

"Oh, very well," said Brelca. "She can join us if she wishes—but don't say I didn't warn you when there's trouble."

"That's settled then," said Spelbush, climbing back into the box. "Consider yourself a member of the crew, miss. Come along, Fistram. We've wasted more time than enough—it's time we were on our way to the coast."

"We can't go *now*," said Ernest.

"I beg your pardon?" said Spelbush.

"*Why* can't we leave now?" asked Fistram.

"Because there'll be every copper and parish officer out searching for Emily for the next two days at least."

"What did I say!" crowed Brelca. "What did I tell you? Didn't I warn that there'd be trouble!"

"We can't stay here either," said Emily. "This graveyard is the first place they'll look."

"We'll have to turn back," said Ernest.

"Turn *back*?" cried Spelbush. "We can't do that! A Lilliputian never turns back."

"We're on our way to the coast," said Fistram. "We

can't go back now."

"Besides," said Brelca, "there's nowhere we can go back to."

"Yes, there is," said Ernest. "Back to that house where we were before."

Spelbush stamped his foot. "Absolutely out of the question! A thousand thousand plumstones upon thy head, boy, for daring to suggest it! *No!* I will not countenance such a move."

"But we *must*," argued Ernest. "We've got to lie low for a day or two. It's only a few streets from here. If we can get back there and get inside and somehow sneak back up to that nursery—"

"As leader of the *Antelope* expedition," said Spelbush, firmly, "I categorically forbid that we turn back."

"All right then," said Ernest. "*You* think of something."

Spelbush scratched his head and thought hard. He looked at Fistram and Brelca who were both staring at him, expectantly. He did not have one single idea in his head.

"On the other hand, of course," said Spelbush, "if we *did* turn back and it *was* only for a day or two . . ."

8

"Stop that girl!" cried Silas Elmwood. "Hold that boy! Seize the pair of them!"

A police constable drew his whistle and blew three short, sharp blasts. A second constable, truncheon in hand, ran down the street in the direction that the children's officer was pointing. The policeman's heavy studded boots clattered on the cobblestones.

"This way!" said Ernest, grabbing Emily by the hand and leading her off round a street corner.

It had been an awful stroke of bad luck.

The two children, with the Lilliputians in the boot-black box, had very nearly made it to the Garstanton house. They had just been turning into the street where the photographer's shop was situated when Elmwood spotted them.

The children's officer, having obtained the assistance of a couple of policemen, was on his way back to search the cemetery when he saw Ernest and Emily.

"You come with me!" Elmwood called to the constable with the whistle, beckoning him the other way. "They can't escape us now—we'll have them trapped around the back."

But when the children's officer and the constable met up with the second policeman in the back street, there was no sign of the children. There were, however, a number of tall green doors set in a long brick wall, opening on to the back gardens of the houses on either side.

"They must be hiding in one of these," growled Elmwood. "Search every one. I'll make the little wretches rue the day they were born for leading us such a jig! You take the gardens on that side, constable," he called, then, turning to the second policeman, he added, "We'll start here."

By chance, the very first door that Elmwood opened led him into the Garstanton back garden. Mr Garstanton was tending his rose bushes. "Are you looking for someone, officer?" asked the old photographer, recognizing Silas Elmwood by his gold-buttoned uniform.

"Aye—that I am," growled Elmwood. "A lad and a lass. The lad's carrying a boot-black box. Two juvenile offenders wanted by the law."

"And what crime are they accused of?"

"The girl has run away from the workhouse, the boy's wanted for assisting her escape—and assaulting me into the bargain." As he spoke, Elmwood touched the lump on his forehead where the garden rake had struck him.

"They're certainly not in my garden, as you can plainly see," said Mr Garstanton. "And they're not in the house— I've been here for the past half hour and nobody has gone past me."

"An' I can vouch for that," said Millie, who had appeared with a basket of washing. "I've been in the wash-'ouse boiling whites all morning—an' there ain't nobody gone through there."

Elmwood frowned. "If either of 'em should turn up, you'll know what's to be done," he said.

"I will indeed, officer," said Mr Garstanton. "You may

be sure that I shall take the appropriate action."

Silas Elmwood nodded, uncertainly. He was not quite sure what the old man meant by his last remark. But there was no time to pursue that further. There were a dozen other gardens to be searched.

"Come on," he snapped at the constable, and turned towards the garden door.

As soon as the two had gone, Mr Garstanton opened the door to the greenhouse. "Out you come, you pair of fugitives from law and order," he said with a smile.

Ernest and Emily came out of the greenhouse looking nervously all around. Ernest clutched tight hold of the box with its precious contents.

"Why, bless my soul!" said Millie. "If it ain't the lad with the boot-black box what that there detective was looking for. But I never thought I'd live to see the day when you was guilty of a whopper, sir."

"A whopper, Millie?"

"Yes, sir—you *knows*, sir—telling a fib, beggin' yer pardin, sir."

"Are you accusing me of speaking an untruth, Millie?"

"Not that I blames you at all for doin' it, sir, but yes, I am. I 'eard you with my own ears telling that there children's officer that you 'adn't clapped eyes on these two kiddies."

"But I did nothing of the kind, Millie. I merely told him that the children he was seeking were not in my garden. Neither they were—they were in my greenhouse. I bundled them both in there myself not ten minutes ago." Then, turning to Ernest, he continued, "Now, you young scallywag, do you believe me when I tell you that I don't mean you any harm?"

Ernest nodded, slowly.

"But if you ain't a-going to turn 'em in, sir," said the housemaid, "what *are* you a-going to do with 'em?"

Mr Garstanton peered keenly at the children and thought hard. "Clean 'em up for a beginning. That's your job, Millie."

"*Mine*, sir?"

"Yours and Cook's. Baths are the first order of the day. Have them as bright and shining as a couple of the Queen's Own Troopers. Then kit them out. If I'm not mistaken, there's a trunk full of my grandchildren's clothes somewhere on the premises. When these two are fit for C.O.'s Parade, march 'em both into the dining room and we'll see about some rations." He turned back to the children and smiled. "You wouldn't say 'no', I don't suppose, to a spot of lunch?"

Ernest and Emily eagerly shook their heads.

The clothes that Millie found for the children fitted both of them perfectly. Ernest kept the boot-black box close beside him on a dining chair as they ate the scrumptious lunch which Cook had provided. He even succeeded in slipping the occasional tasty morsel into the box without Mr Garstanton noticing.

When the old gentleman rang for Millie, the housemaid gaped in wonder at the empty plates and dishes.

"Well now!" she said. "I reckons I ain't never knowed nothing disappear so fast in my entire life!"

"And they both feel better for it, I'll be bound," said Mr Garstanton.

The children nodded as they both let out a contented sigh.

"What I wants to know, sir, is what you're a-going to do wiv 'em now that they're both tidied up and fed fit to bust?"

"Exactly the problem that's been puzzling me, Millie," said Mr Garstanton, frowning thoughtfully. "There's no furniture in the nursery—I suppose we could fit them both, temporarily, in the spare bedroom."

Millie's mouth dropped open. "Why, sir, you ain't intendin' to *keep* 'em surely?"

"Why not? What else did you imagine I was going to do?"

"But they ain't yours to keep, sir!"

"Then whose are they, may I ask? Emily here tells me that she's a refugee from the workhouse—you're not suggesting that I send her back there, I hope?"

"No, sir! 'Course not! As if I would!"

"And as for Ernest—"

"I've runned away from 'ome," Ernest explained to Millie.

"Precisely," said Mr Garstanton. "And why? Because the poor little lad was being led a dog's life."

"All the same," said Millie, doubtfully, "badly treated there or not, 'e 'as got a 'ome to go to . . ."

"No, I haven't," said Ernest. "Not a *real* home. I lived with this old woman who called herself my grannie—but she wasn't my *real* grannie. I only called her that. Same as I called the feller I was with before my uncle—and the woman afore that, my aunt. I wasn't really related to any of them. I haven't got no real relatives I knows about. I'm an orphan really, just like Emm."

"There, you see, Millie," said Mr Garstanton. "Another candidate for the workhouse."

"But that don't mean to say that you can keep 'em 'ere, sir, bless your heart. There's police and that there children's officer searching 'igh and low for 'em. They'll track 'em down to 'ere sooner or later, you mark my words they will. They'll find 'em 'ere within the week."

"Then they won't *be* here, Millie," replied Mr Garstanton, arriving at a sudden decision. "Until something can be arranged about their future, I shall take these children away somewhere where they can't be found."

"But take 'em *where*, sir?" asked the puzzled housemaid.

Mr Garstanton pondered on the vexing problem. "I don't know," he said at last. "Somewhere that will put some roses in their pale cheeks, Millie—and you shall come as well! I haven't quite decided where that is yet . . ." He paused, scratched at his chin and turned to Emily and Ernest. "But I'll wager you won't turn your noses up at the seaside, eh?"

The sea!

Ernest and Emily exchanged a joyful glance.

The *sea!*

Inside the boot-black box, the Lilliputians shook hands with each other triumphantly.

It was what they all had wanted all the time.

The *sea!*

"Yes, please!" said Ernest and Emily in unison.

Mr Garstanton raised his glass of sherry again. "The seaside it is then!" he announced.

The children raised their lemonade glasses.

Mr Garstanton could see that Millie was also excited at the prospect, but that she was without a drink in her hand. "You're included too, Millie," he said. "Get yourself a glass."

"May I, sir?"

"I insist!"

Millie poured herself a glass of lemonade from the big jug on the table. All four of them raised their glasses.

"Here's to it!" said Mr Garstanton.

"The seaside!" cried Emily and Ernest.

Inside the boot-black box, the little people were without drinks to toast the occasion, but they mouthed the words along with the children.

Millie grinned. "The seaside," she said, "and all them what sails on it!"

Mr Garstanton was as good as his word.

The very next day, quite early in the morning, the children found themselves at the railway station together with their new-found benefactor and Millie, the housemaid. The boot-black box, as always, was tucked safely under Ernest's arm.

The train was waiting for them at the platform.

The photographer and Millie stacked the luggage on the rack in the compartment while the children took themselves off to the penny chocolate bar machine. It was the very first time that either Emily or Ernest had been inside a railway station and the first time too that they had seen such a machine. It took them some time to understand how it worked.

"If those two children don't get a move on, Millie," said Mr Garstanton, peering out of the compartment window, "we'll be off to the coast without them—tell 'em they're wanted on parade."

"Very good, sir," said Millie. She unbuckled the thick leather strap and lowered the window in the door. "Miss Emily! Master Ernest!" she called across the platform. "I 'opes as 'ow you pair knows that this train's abaht ready to set off!"

"Just coming!" Ernest called back.

"Shan't be a minute, Millie!" cried Emily.

As Millie put her head back inside the compartment, Ernest succeeded at last in pushing home the coin-slide and getting his penny chocolate bar.

"All aboard!" shouted the guard, shooting the children a cautionary glance as he walked along the platform towards the rear end of the train.

Ernest handed Emily the boot-black box and struggled with the silver wrapping-paper on the bar of chocolate.

"Get a move on, boy!" snapped Spelbush, peering over the top of the box as Emily opened the lid.

"I'm being as fast as I can," said Ernest.

"We'll miss the train," squealed Fistram. "I *know* we will!"

"If we do, it will be all your fault, Fistram," snapped Brelca. "It was you who wanted something to eat in the first place!"

"Then you should thank me for thinking of it!" said Fistram, turning up his nose at Spelbush. "Had it been left to *some* people, we'd have been setting out for the sea without any rations at all."

Ernest had finally managed to unwrap the chocolate bar and was now breaking it up into pieces.

"Do *hurry*, Ernie," said Emily, glancing anxiously at the clouds of steam hissing from between the engine's wheels.

"Here, grab hold of these," said Ernest, handing out blocks of chocolate to the Lilliputians who seized them in both arms.

Fistram looked down at the giant-sized piece of chocolate

he was grasping and pulled a face. "It's plain," he grumbled. "You didn't tell me that it was *plain*. You know very well how much I detest plain chocolate."

"Oh, do stop complaining, Fistram, and do sit down!" said Emily. As she spoke, she closed the lid of the box on the little people.

She had acted just in time.

"Sharp's the word, you spadgers!" said a voice at Ernest's elbow. A porter was standing right beside them. "If you're not going to miss your train, you'd better run for it!"

Along the platform, the guard was blowing his whistle and waving his green flag.

"Come along then!" cried the porter, adding obligingly, "I'll take that, miss!"

Before she knew what was happening, the porter had lifted the boot-black box out of Emily's hands.

Ernest, Emily and the porter ran across the platform to where Millie was holding open the compartment door. The housemaid gave a helping hand as the porter bundled first Emily and then Ernest inside. As soon as they were both safely in, Mr Garstanton pulled hard on the door.

"The box!" cried Emily in alarm.

Ernest turned quickly but now both door and window were shut tight. Outside, on the platform, the porter was holding up the box.

"Oh no!" cried Ernest. "Get it, quick!"

"Open the door!" said Mr Garstanton.

"I can't," said Millie, fumbling with the door handle. "It's stuck fast."

"Here—let me," said Mr Garstanton.

Millie moved aside and the photographer unbuckled the

thick leather strap securing the window.

But the train was already rumbling forward.

Outside, on the platform, the porter could see the children's agonized faces. Mr Garstanton slid down the window in the door at last.

It was too late.

"Don't worry!" yelled the porter, as the train began to pick up speed. "I'll give it to the guard!"

True to his word, the porter passed the boot-black box through the window of the guard's van as the rear portion of the train swept past him.

Mr Garstanton turned back into the compartment. "Problem solved," he said to the children. "There's nothing for you to worry about. It'll be quite safe in the guard's van. We'll collect it when we arrive at our destination."

Emily and Ernest, concerned for the well-being of their little friends, exchanged a worried look. But there was nothing to be done. There was no corridor on the train and therefore no way that they could get to the guard's van. They could only wait and hope that what Mr Garstanton had said was true.

"Anyways, I dunno why you 'as to carry that box abaht with you everywheres, Master Ernest," said Millie, with a grin, "there ain't no shoes wants cleaning in this compartment."

But the children could manage no more than wan smiles in reply to Millie's joking. They settled themselves in their seats, as comfortably as they could, in readiness for the long journey that lay ahead.

At the back of the train, in the guard's van, the boot-black box vibrated gently on top of the packing-case where the guard had put it. He had then retired to the other end of his van to read his newspaper.

Inside the boot-black box, the little people pondered over their predicament. On the bustling, noisy railway-station platform, with the lid shut tight, it had been difficult to hear—and difficult to understand what was going on.

They had felt, rather than heard, the porter take possession of the box. They had also been aware of the jogging up and down they'd had in the race to catch the train. But of what had happened after that, they were not quite sure—although they had a good idea that they were no longer in the safekeeping of the children.

"Where do you think we are?" asked Fistram, nervously.

"Wherever we are, Fistram, it's all your fault," snapped Brelca. "You and your penny chocolate bar!"

There was only one way, Spelbush decided, to find out exactly what had happened to them. And that was to take a look. Spelbush got down on his hands and knees and motioned to Fistram to clamber up on to his back and peer out of the lid.

Fistram did so.

What he saw caused him some concern. Looking down over the edge of the packing-case and on to the floor of the guard's van, Fistram could see a row of enormous cages. Each cage contained one or two or even several giant-sized animals—giant-sized, that is, to the tiny Lilliputian. Enormous clucking brown hens; gigantic squealing piglets snuffling on a bed of straw; two huge white rabbits, both as big as elephants—and, most frightening of all, beyond the cages, tethered by a rope, a black-and-white billy goat of mammoth proportions.

Fistram gulped and ducked down into the box.

"Well?" asked Spelbush. "Where are we then?"

"We . . . we seem to have been put into some sort of travelling monster zoo!" stammered Fistram.

Spelbush sighed and shook his head. "You take a look, Brelca," he said.

Brelca stepped up on to Spelbush's back, pushed the lid up slightly and stared out. A moment later she was back on the floor of the box. "It's only livestock," she said. "We're in the guard's van."

"Travelling monster zoo indeed!" said Spelbush, giving Fistram a scornful glance. "Well then," he continued, "it would seem that we are going to be here for quite some time—we might as well make the best of things."

Spelbush tucked himself down in a corner of the box, picked up a block of chocolate in both hands, bit a lump out of it and then passed it on to Brelca.

Brelca also took a bite and then offered it to Fistram.

"No, thank you, Brelca. I don't like plain chocolate."

"There's nothing else," said Brelca.

"Eat, Fistram," ordered Spelbush. "Who knows what perils lie ahead? We must keep our strength up."

"Oh, very well," sighed Fistram, taking the chocolate block from Brelca, and nibbling at the edge.

Back in the Garstanton compartment, Ernest and Emily had both dropped off to sleep. They were curled up opposite each other in two of the window-seats.

"In the Land of Nod, bless 'em," said Millie to Mr Garstanton. "They was that excited at goin' to the seaside, they was up and washed and dressed afore the crack of dawn."

"And how about you, Millie?" said Mr Garstanton, looking over the top of *The Times*. "Are you excited at the

114

prospect of the seaside too?"

"I'm looking forward to the seaside again, sir, yes—but I ain't lookin' forward one little bit to goin' back to that there boardin'-house, an' that's a fact." Millie paused and gave a little shiver. "It fair gives me the goose-bumps just to think of that Miss Mincing!"

Mr Garstanton had written off for lodgings at the same boarding-house where he and his grandchildren had stayed the year before: the same boarding-house where Millie Lottersby had been employed as a maid—or should one say a household drudge?—by Sarah Mincing, before getting the sack and taking up employment with the kind-hearted photographer; the very same boarding-house, in fact, where the *Antelope* adventure had begun. But all that had been a long time ago.

Mr Garstanton smiled and shook his head. "Miss Mincing, Millie, has not been near her boarding-house in months and months," he said.

The photographer, of course, was completely unaware that both Miss Mincing and her brother had been breathing down his neck for almost a year, in pursuit of the little people who lived beneath his roof—and also without his knowledge.

"Miss Mincing has leased her boarding-house business to someone else—I have that on the very best authority, Millie," continued Mr Garstanton. "Nobody knows where the Mincings went."

"That may be so, sir—but I slaved my fingers to the bone in that there boarding-'ouse, an' it ain't easy to forget it!"

"All the more reason, Millie, for you to enjoy yourself there now the second time around—and one of the reasons why I've arranged for us all to stay there. Being a guest in the house, Millie, will help to dispel any unhappy memories you still harbour from your days there as a household slave."

But Millie was not too sure. "If you sez so, sir, I suppose it's right," she replied, doubtfully.

"And I *do* say so! All that will be required of you will be to get the children on parade in time and so on—see that they clean their teeth and comb their hair and suchlike. Keep 'em amused and entertained and so forth. Relief of Mafeking on the sands, eh? Charge of the Light Brigade on the seaside donkeys! You'll have no end of a time!"

"Lor' love you, sir, but you ain't a-gettin' me up on no donkey!" said Millie, managing a smile at last. She glanced at the two children who were still sleeping peacefully. "Still, as long as they enjoys *them*selves, innit? If you could've seen the pair of 'em this morning! There they was, gettin' their own breakfasts afore anyone else in the 'ouse 'ad stirred! Then the both of them sitting at the kitchen table with that there boot-box in front of 'em!"

"They carry that box around with them as if it contained a Rajah's ransom," said Mr Garstanton.

"I often wonders what they 'ave got in it—'cos they won't let nobody so much as peep inside. 'Ere! Their faces, eh, when they 'eard as 'ow it was 'avin' to travel in the guard's van!"

Mr Garstanton chuckled at the thought. Had it not been for fear of waking Emily and Ernest, he would have laughed out loud. He smiled across dotingly at his two young charges. He was looking forward to the seaside trip as much as anyone—but more for the children's sake than

116

his own. They were about to enjoy the time of their lives, he told himself.

Happy at the thought, the photographer returned to reading his newspaper while Millie watched the countryside flash past outside the window.

The train was now rattling along at top speed as it headed towards the coast.

9

Although it did not disturb the guard, who had nodded off and was snoring loudly, the unsteady motion of the train was having a distinct effect on the boot-black box. The increased vibration, now that the train was travelling at full speed, was causing the box to shudder slowly across the top of the packing-case it was resting on.

One of the Lilliputians inside the box recognized what was happening.

"We're moving!" said Fistram, in some alarm.

"Of course we're moving, Fistram," said Brelca. "We're on a moving train—it's taking us to the sea, remember?"

"I'm not talking about the train we're travelling on," replied Fistram. "This box is on the move as well. It *is* Spelbush—I can *feel* it!"

"Stand quite still, the pair of you," said Spelbush, who had a funny feeling that, for once, Fistram could be right. "Let me judge for myself."

The three Lilliputians stood like statues for several seconds. While they did so, the box moved closer and closer to the edge of the packing-case. In fact, a couple of centimetres of one end of the box now over-hung the edge of the case. Before long, the box would go crashing to the floor below.

"It's true, you know!" said Spelbush with a frown. "We

are moving—quite definitely. Have another look outside, Brelca." Spelbush got down on all fours and invited Brelca to clamber on his back.

But as Brelca stepped forward there was a sudden unsteady movement under her feet. Almost half the box had now vibrated over the edge of the packing-case and the combined weight of the two Lilliputians had caused the box to tip up.

"Get back! Retreat!" urged Spelbush, sensing what had happened.

Brelca and Spelbush hurled themselves towards the far end of the box where Fistram was standing. The boot-black box steadied, but there was no time to be lost. The bottom of the box continued to vibrate beneath their feet. With Fistram's help, Brelca clambered up on to Spelbush's shoulders.

"Push!" cried Spelbush. "Push hard!"

Brelca put both hands against the lid and pushed with all her strength. Slowly, the lid rose upwards and finally opened. Brelca eased herself from Spelbush's shoulders and sat astride the end wall of the box.

Now it was Fistram's turn. With Brelca giving him a hand from above and Spelbush pushing from below, Fistram was soon sitting beside Brelca. The two of them pulled Spelbush up to join them.

While this had been going on, the box had continued to move. At any moment it might fall.

"Jump!" cried Spelbush.

As one, the three Lilliputians leapt down on to the packing-case. Without the weight of the little people to hold it, the boot-black box tipped and fell to the floor of the guard's van with a heavy thud.

The noise disturbed the guard from his slumbers. Waking with a start, he got to his feet and walked the length of the van towards the sound. But this gave Spelbush sufficient time to lead his companions over the far edge of the packing-case to temporary safety. They lowered themselves on to the top of a second crate, where they were safely hidden from the eyes of the guard.

Stooping to pick up the empty boot-black box, the guard put it on a shelf high on the side of the van. Satisfied that it was now secure, the guard walked back to his desk. It was time, he decided, to catch up on some paperwork.

The three Lilliputians stared up at the box now high above their heads.

"We'll never get back inside again," said Spelbush mournfully.

"Oh well," said Brelca, shrugging her shoulders. "Who cares?"

"I do, Brelca," said Fistram. "I was beginning to get very attached to that box—it was starting to feel like home."

"It never felt like home to *me*," snapped Brelca. "It was always full of your biscuit crumbs for one thing—and it wasn't big enough for another. It was like living in a shoe-box."

"It *is* a shoe-box," Spelbush pointed out. "Or a boot-box, at least—there isn't very much difference. But that's not the point, Brelca. If we're not back inside that box when this train arrives at its destination, we won't meet up with those children again and—"

"Look out!" cried Fistram.

The guard was walking back along the van with a sheaf of documents in his hand. He moved slowly, checking the goods that were in his care.

"This way!" said Spelbush, setting off across the top of the crate.

Getting down to floor-level did not prove difficult. There were any number of various sized cardboard cartons, drums of paint and brown-paper packages. It was easy to scramble from one to the other. In next to no time, they were standing on the van's wooden planking.

But it was then, with their feet planted safely on the floor, that their troubles began.

Suddenly, and without warning, the guard's feet appeared round a box of oranges. Momentarily panic-stricken, the three Lilliputians took flight.

Rounding the bottom of a milk-churn, Spelbush jerked open the catch on a wire-meshed door and slipped inside, followed by Fistram. The two Lilliputians found themselves in the cage containing two white rabbits. But the occupants of the cage seemed not at all concerned at the arrival of the two intruders. The rabbits twitched their noses inquisitively at Fistram and Spelbush and then returned to nibbling at some lettuce leaves on the floor of the cage. The Lilliputians breathed again, but then Spelbush's face clouded over with concern.

"Where's Brelca?" he demanded.

Fistram shook his head. He had not the faintest idea.

In the headlong rush for cover, Brelca had taken off in a different direction and had managed to squeeze herself through the bars of one of the cages on the other side of the van. But she had not been so lucky in her choice of hiding-place.

Feeling loose straw beneath her feet and hearing squeals and sniffles, Brelca had discovered, to her horror and disgust, that she had taken refuge in a crate full of piglets.

Before she had time to escape, she found herself being pushed and shoved and buffeted by the animals. Although they were only weeks old, to Brelca they seemed like a herd of rampaging pink rhinoceroses. To save herself from being trampled underfoot, she wriggled her way across the cage and stood with her back pressed to one side of the crate.

"Get back, you ugly beast!" she stormed, as a particularly inquisitive piglet push its snout against her stomach.

"Brelca! Over here!" It was Fistram's voice.

"This way, Brelca!"

Turning her head and looking out through the bars of the crate, she could just make out her two companions waving at her through a wire-mesh door. By edging her body sidewards, Brelca was able to poke and prod her way past the piglets and back to the bars. Thankfully, she squeezed her body out again.

Glancing quickly to either side, and seeing no sign of the guard, Brelca scampered across to the wire-mesh door which Fistram was holding open for her.

She pulled up short when she realized that Spelbush and Fistram were sharing the cage with two large white rabbits.

"Are they . . . are they safe?" she asked.

Spelbush laughed. "*Safe?*" he echoed. "They're *rabbits*, Brelca—rabbits as big as elephants I'll grant you—but rabbits all the same. Of course they're safe."

"I have just escaped, by the skin of my teeth, from a litter of giant-sized piglets! If you had suffered that experience, Spelbush, you'd be wary of a new-born mouse."

"There is nothing to fear in here, Brelca," said Spelbush, throwing himself down on the soft straw under the nose of an uninterested rabbit.

Brelca yawned and lay on the straw herself.

"Would either of you care for a piece of carrot?" asked Fistram, who had discovered just such a thing hidden underneath a lettuce leaf. "I don't think the rabbits have nibbled it *very* much."

"Certainly not," said Spelbush.

"No, thank you!" said Brelca, yawning again. Her adventure with the piglets had tired her out, she decided. Closing her eyes, she settled down for some well-earned sleep.

The train rattled along the track. The *clickety-click*, *clickety-click* it made as it sped along the rails was a soothing sound sufficient to put many of the passengers to sleep. In the Garstanton compartment, Millie and her employer had both dozed off, and it was not long before Brelca, Spelbush and Fistram were also fast asleep on the floor of the rabbit-hutch.

As the hours passed, only the guard stayed awake in his van, hard at work with the papers and documents on his desk.

The engine's whistle let out a shrill toot which signified that they were nearing the coast. The guard took out his silver watch and checked the time. It would not be long now before they arrived at their destination. The guard eased himself from off his tall stool and walked along his van, checking the contents for the last time.

"Hullo," he said softly, glancing down. "What's this then?" He had noticed that the catch of the door to the rabbit hutch was unfastened. He bent down and slipped it into place. "Good job I noticed that," he congratulated himself, and then moved on again.

Inside the hutch, the three Lilliputians slept on, unaware

that the door had been locked.

Back in the compartment, Mr Garstanton's slumbers were disturbed by three more blasts from the engine-whistle. The photographer blinked, peered out of the window and cleared his throat. "Time to start getting things together," he observed to Millie, who had also woken with a start.

"Come on, you sleepy-heads!" said the housemaid, giving both Emily and Ernest a little shake.

The children woke immediately, both filled with excitement.

They stared out of the windows. The countryside had given way to row upon row of neat, white-walled cottages. The train slowed down as it approached the flower-bordered platforms of the seaside railway station.

They had arrived!

The station master and the porter were waiting on the platform for the carriage doors to open and the holiday-makers to emerge.

Inside the Garstanton compartment, Millie helped Emily and Ernest into their outdoor coats. Mr Garstanton poked his head out of the window and beckoned the porter to help with the luggage. All along the train, doors were opening and passengers were stepping down on to the platform.

Emily and Ernest were among the first off the train. Anxious for the safety of their little friends they ran along the platform as fast as their legs would carry them, back to where the guard was unloading the contents of his van on to a waiting hand-truck.

"Can I have my box, please?" Ernest asked the guard.

"Hold your horses, young 'un!" said the guard, good-naturedly. He had just stepped out of his van with the rabbit-hutch held firmly in both hands. He lowered the hutch safely on to the truck and then turned back to the children. "Now then, what was it you was wanting?" he asked.

"Our box," said Emily, holding out her hands. "It's about so big and it's got a handle on the top."

"I know the one," said the guard, snapping his fingers. "I put it up on a shelf for safety. I'm afraid it took a bit of a tumble earlier on when it fell off a packing-case. Still, being a boot-black's box, I don't suppose there's anything inside it what could come to any harm? Hang on—I'll fetch it for you." As he disappeared inside the van, Emily and Ernest looked at one another in horror. They did not notice the three Lilliputians furiously trying to attract their attention by waving through the wire-mesh on the door of the rabbit-hutch.

"Here we are then!" said the guard, re-appearing with the boot-box in his hands. "One boot-box, cleaning for the use of!"

"Thanks very much," said Ernest, quckly taking the box from the guard's grasp.

Emily held her breath as Ernest lifted the lid.

His face fell.

"Are they all right?" asked Emily, anxiously.

Ernest shook his head. "They're not here," he said. "They've gone."

"Gone *where?*"

Ernest turned back to the train, but the guard, having put out all the goods to be delivered, had locked his van and was walking off.

Some yards away, inside the rabbit-hutch, the three little people continued to wave and call to the children. But to no avail. Ernest and Emily made their way back along the platform, downcast. They neither saw nor heard the Lilliputians on the truck behind them.

When they arrived back at the compartment, the children found Mr Garstanton and Millie standing on the platform with the luggage.

"I see you've got that old box back safe and sound?" said the housemaid with a grin. The children made no reply. Their shoulders drooped as they stared sadly down at the platform. "My, my, my!" teased Millie. "We ain't 'arf feeling sorry for ourselves then, ain't we? Cheer up, you two! You're on your 'olidays, supposed to be!"

The children were not alone in being out of humour. Mr Garstanton had so far failed in his attempt to attract the attention of the station's porter which made him feel rather cross. "I say! You there!" he called out as the porter came along the platform.

"Yes, sir?" said the man, touching his cap and acknowledging the photographer at last.

"Give me a hand with these, would you?" said Mr Garstanton, waving his umbrella at the collection of bags and cases on the platform.

"Right away, sir!" replied the porter, bringing up the partly loaded hand-truck he had just collected from outside the guard's van.

It was Emily who noticed the three little faces peering angrily through the rabbit-hutch door. She nudged Ernest, and while Mr Garstanton, Millie and the porter busied themselves loading the luggage on to the hand-truck, the children stooped and peered through the wire mesh.

"Well, don't just stand there—" hissed Spelbush.

"—Grinning like a pair of Lilliputian llamas—" added Fistram.

Emily and Ernest, amused at finding the little people locked away with a pair of bright-eyed, pink-nosed rabbits, hid their smiles and helped the Lilliputians out of the hutch and back into the safety of the boot-black box.

The afternoon sun shone down on a blue and shimmering sea that broke along an empty expanse of golden sand stretching as far as eye could see.

"Hecky moses!" gasped Ernest. "So *that's* what the sea looks like!"

"Isn't it . . . isn't it *grand*!" sighed Emily, filled with wonder at the sight.

The children, together with Mr Garstanton and Emily, were sitting in a horse-drawn open carriage. Mr Garstanton had asked the cabman to pull up for a minute or two so that the children might savour their first glimpse of the sea. They were on their way to the boarding-house and the luggage was on a rack at the back of the carriage—with the exception of the boot-black box on Ernest's lap.

The little people, of course, were safe inside the box.

"It goes on for ever and ever!" said Ernest, unable to take his eyes from the gently rolling sea.

"And just look at all that sand!" cried Emily, adding anxiously, "It won't all get washed away before we have a chance to play on it, will it?"

"There'll be more than enough for both of you," said Mr Garstanton with a chuckle. "But first things first, eh? Time we presented ourselves at our lodgings. Still nervous about arriving, Millie?"

"No, sir," said Millie with determination. "Not if you

says that old Ma Mincing ain't there no longer, sir."

"Take my word for it, Millie—she moved on months ago. Drive on, cabbie!"

The cabman cracked his whip and the horse and carriage moved off again along the promenade.

10

"I don't believe it!" gasped Sarah Mincing, staring through the lace curtains at the window of her parlour. "I simply *refuse* to believe it!"

"Refuse to believe what, Sarah?" asked Harwell, who was sitting in an easy chair with his long legs sprawled out in front of the fire.

"Oh, do stop lounging and get up on your feet, brother! You're creasing my antimacassar—to say nothing of soiling it with your foul-smelling, heathen Turkish hair-oil!" Sarah paused and looked again at the horse-drawn open carriage which was drawing up outside the front door. "I don't believe it—and yet it's true! Pass me that penny-post envelope—*quickly!*—over there on the bureau."

Harwell rose to his feet and ambled across to pick up the letter.

Sarah Mincing had returned to her boarding-house only the day before. She had finally had her fill of pursuing the little people. The summer season was about to get under way and there was more money to be made in fleecing holiday-makers, she told herself, than she would ever earn from something that existed only in her brother's fevered mind. Harwell Mincing, having no means of support apart from that which he could beg, borrow or filch from his sister's purse, had been forced to accompany his sister and give up his dreams of ensnaring the cunning creatures—at least for the time being.

"Here you are, Sarah," said Harwell, handing his sister the penny-post envelope which had arrived that morning. As he spoke, Harwell glanced over an aspidistra through the window. His eyes opened wide with astonishment at what he saw outside. "The old billy-goat's here!" he cried. "*And* the boot-black urchin! *And* the boot-black box itself, praise be!"

"And Millie Lottersby too, the idle slattern! I knew there was a party of four concerned, but I didn't bother to read the name —" Sarah had taken the letter out of the envelope, unfolded it, and now studied the signature at the bottom. " 'Ralph Garstanton'—it *is* from him!"

"But don't you realize what this means, sister?" said Harwell, triumphantly.

"I realize all too well," snapped Sarah. "I have arrived back at my own residence after pursuing the wildest of wild-goose chases all these months— only to find the very same wild-goose chase turn up on my very own doorstep!"

Harwell shook his head. "Nay, Sarah," he said, "it means that heaven has chosen to smile down upon us at last!"

"Watch thy tongue, brother!" said Sarah, sharply. "Be careful of thy blaspheming!"

"But it has, sister, it *has*!" insisted Harwell. "I *said* that the old goat knew more about the little creatures than he cared to pretend. I *told* you that the boot-black urchin was no figment of my imagination. I *knew* that the boot-black box would one day drop into our lap! It means that fame and fortune are about to fall upon us, Sarah!"

Sarah Mincing glanced out of the window again. "It also

means that you had best get yourself down into the kitchen, Harwell," she said. "They've almost unloaded the luggage."

"How right you are, sister," said Harwell, for once agreeing with Sarah. "The old goat has seen me too many times in too many disguises to see me now as I am. I'll hide myself this instant."

"Nay, brother, I was not concerned with your concealment," said Sarah with a sniff. "If I'm to attend to a party of four lodgers under my roof—and I'm without a single servant in the house—then someone must needs attend to the cooking. Get yourself below stairs, Harwell, and put an apron round yourself."

"An *apron*, sister?" said Harwell, aghast. "*Me?*"

"You heard me, brother. If you wish me to keep you, then you must earn your living like all the rest of the world. *At once!*"

Harwell crept off dolefully. He dared not disobey his sister.

Outside in the street, meanwhile, the cabman had unloaded the luggage from the rack at the back of the carriage.

"Thank you, cabbie," said Mr Garstanton, handing the cabman his fare and a sizeable tip.

"Thank *you*, guvnor!"

The cabman clambered back up on his driving-seat, took up the reins and "clucked" his tongue between his teeth. The horse tugged at the shafts and the carriage rumbled off along the street.

"Well, well, well," said the photographer, softly, turning to study the front of the house. "But this brings back a few memories!" He was thinking of the good times he had shared with his grandchildren.

"I daresay it does, sir, for both of us," said Millie, who had her own memories of the boarding-house where she had previously been employed by Sarah Mincing. "But I can't swear to 'em being pleasant, and that's a fact!"

"Now, Millie, I promise you that there's nothing to fear," said Mr Garstanton, as he approached the entrance. "Come, children—"

But the front door was opened from inside before his hand had touched the bell-pull.

"Good-day to you, Mr Garstanton," said Miss Mincing, staring at him frostily, her thin hands clasped across her black dress.

"Why, Miss M-m-m-mincing—" stammered Mr Garstanton, amazed to see her. "We were given to understand that you were no longer in residence here?"

"Which just goes to prove, Mr Garstanton, that one should set little store by idle gossip," said Sarah Mincing coldly, flashing the housemaid a disapproving glance. "Well then, are you going to bring your luggage inside, or am I expected to stand here all afternoon with my front door wide open, allowing the dust and dirt to blow into the household willy-nilly?"

Mr Garstanton's surprise at being confronted by Sarah Mincing prevented him from making any immediate reply. His mouth opened and closed soundlessly. He cast an apologetic glance at Millie, who looked more dismayed than he was at finding her ex-employer back at the boarding-house. But there was nothing he could do to ease her unhappiness at that moment.

"Come along, children," he said, finding his tongue at last. "Help me to carry the luggage."

Mr Garstanton, Millie, Emily and Ernest all picked up

cases of varying sizes and trooped despondently through the front door.

The holiday could not possibly have got off to a worse start!

Later that same evening, after the guests had eaten a frugal supper in the dining room, Harwell Mincing sat at the kitchen table peeling potatoes for the following day. Sarah bustled into the kitchen, having just been upstairs to make sure that the two children weren't making finger-marks on her wallpaper or scuffing their shoes on the parlour floorboards.

Harwell glanced up eagerly at Sarah's entrance and then frowned when he saw that she was empty-handed. "Haven't you managed to relieve those brats of that boot-box yet?" he muttered crossly.

"Fiddle-faddle to the boot-box, Harwell," snapped Sarah. "I've more important things than boot-boxes on my mind—haven't *you* finished those potatoes yet?"

"I'm being as quick as I can, sister. I wasn't brought into this world to be a kitchen skivvy."

"No!" stormed Sarah. "And I wasn't brought into this world to be a kitchen skivvy's skivvy either!"

"What kitchen skivvy's skivvy?" asked Harwell, surprised at the depth of anger in Sarah's voice.

"Why, that Millie Lottersby's, who else? I'd had enough of that slovenly flibbertigibbet when I had her in my employ—wasting my money, slapping on blacklead like a bricklayer slaps on mortar!"

"Devil take the girl, Sarah!" snarled Harwell. "Can't you forget her for a single second?"

"Forget her?" cried Sarah. "Forget her! How can I forget her when she's back under my very own roof!

Warming herself in front of *my* fire! She'll sleep tonight in a bed that *I* have had to make! Staying here as a guest! Expecting me to wait upon her hand and foot as if she were some kind of highborn lady—when all the time she knows that I know that she's nothing but a common, feckless, idle slattern!" Sarah paused and rubbed her hands together as the anger built up inside her. "Aye, and not only her—but there's that pair of brats to boot!" she continued. "The boy belongs in the gutter while it's as plain as a pikestaff that the girl's as common as a pigpoke! And as for the old fool of a photographer that had the gall to bring them here . . . I tell you, Harwell, my mind's made up—the four of them may sleep inside these walls tonight but, business or no business, tomorrow morning they can seek fresh lodgings."

"Whatever you say, Sarah," said Harwell with a shrug. "Tonight is all the time that I shall require to get my hands on those mannikins." While they had been talking, Harwell had finished the potatoes and was now pouring out two glasses of milk. "Here, give the brats their supper milk," he said, proffering the glasses at Sarah. "Let's see them off to bed."

"Give them milk?" cried Sarah, raising her hands in horror. "Now I *know* that you are out of your mind, Harwell! Do you imagine that milk grows on trees? If the brats are thirsty, there is water in the tap."

Harwell smiled a crafty smile. "But milk will help them sleep, Sarah," he said. "And while they are in the Land of Nod I plan to steal into their room and get my hands upon the little folk. Is not two glasses of milk a meagre price to pay for such a bargain?"

"Little folk again, is it?" sighed Sarah. "Oh, Harwell—Harwell—if only there was a price upon your sanity—I would skimp and scratch and save to pay it, if only for poor, dear Mother's memory."

Harwell scowled. He resented the suggestion that he was not right in the head. "Take them their milk, sister," he said, curtly. "Upon my oath, before this night is out I shall prove to you beyond any doubt that I am in full possession of my senses!"

Two empty milk-rimmed glasses stood on the cabinet between the beds where Ernest and Emily lay fast asleep. Not a sound came from the boot-black box which lay under Ernest's bed. It had been a long, hard day. The children had been up since dawn that morning. It would take a great deal to disturb their slumber.

And the children were not alone in being tired out by the long train-ride. In a room across the landing, Mr Garstanton was snoring gently in his white night-gown, his night-cap pulled down firmly over his ears. While in a tiny room on the floor above, Millie Lottersby was also fast asleep, dreaming about a soldier-boy that she was yet to meet.

The boarding-house stood still and silent—except for the steady "Tick-tock" from the grandfather clock in the wood-panelled hall.

The door to the kitchen opened slowly and Harwell came into the hall carrying an oil-lamp turned down low. Sarah Mincing followed close at her brother's shoulder. A loose floorboard squeaked under Sarah's patent black-leather boot.

"Quietly does it, sister!" whispered Harwell. "Softlee, softlee, catchee monkey!"

"I fail to understand, brother, why I must needs go about in my own home on tippy-toe—like some sort of common thief," hissed Sarah.

"Thieves we may be, Sarah," said Harwell with a low chuckle. "But we seek an *un*common prize—and a precious one at that! We'll be millionaires tomorrow. Trust me, sister. Have faith."

"*Trust* you?" scoffed Sarah. "Have *faith* in you? Why—I'd as soon put my trust and faith in a whirling dervish!"

"Ssshhh!" Harwell's forefinger went to his lips as he led the way up the stairs. The glow from his oil-lamp was reflected in the bright black eyes of the stuffed birds in the glass cases on the landing. "Take this," he said, handing the lamp to Sarah as they reached the children's bedroom.

The door opened quietly at his touch and they went inside. Sarah held the lamp above her head, shielding the light from the children's faces with her free hand. Harwell searched the room, at first without success.

"I told you, you'd find nothing," whispered Sarah.

"They're in here somewhere, I tell you," Harwell whispered back. "You saw them bring the box inside the house. It *must* be here. They have it hidden somewhere—" He broke off as he finally spotted the boot-black box under Ernest's bed. "There it is!" he hissed triumphantly, pointing.

"Get it then—quickly—and let's get out of here!"

But Harwell was in no hurry. He had waited a long time for the moment when he would hold the little people in his hands. Now that moment had arrived, he was going to savour it to the full. Also, he had no wish to disturb the cunning creatures who, he guessed, were sleeping as soundly in the box as the two brats in their beds. Harwell lifted up the box ever so gently and then, cradling it carefully in his arms, moved towards the door.

Once out on the landing again, with the children's bedroom door closed firmly behind them, Harwell held the box up close to his face. "Fear not, my little ones, my precious ones," he crooned. "Harwell Mincing knows how to take care of his little mannikins! I shall make you famous, my tiny dears, and in return you shall make my fortune!"

"*Our* fortunes, brother," said Sarah, curtly. "And hold your tongue until we're back downstairs or you'll wake the house!"

Harwell closed the kitchen door behind them and set the box down on the table. Taking the oil-lamp back from Sarah he turned up the wick and put it beside the box. Then, in gleeful anticipation of what was to come, he sat down.

"Well, Harwell?" said Sarah, puzzled. "Aren't you going to open it?"

Harwell shook his head and smiled. "Nay, sister," he said. "You've doubted the existence of my miniature people all these months—aye, and questioned my sanity as well—it will give me the greatest pleasure now to allow *you* to open the box. I want to see your face when you are forced to eat your words."

"Very well," said Sarah, sourly. "If that is what you wish." She put out a hand to throw open the lid.

"Gently, Sarah!" said Harwell. "Gently does it! We don't want the cunning little devils to leap out and escape!"

Sarah lifted the lid slowly. Harwell kept his eyes fixed on his sister's face as she peered inside the box. But her face told him nothing. Her mouth remained tight shut.

"How many of them are there, sister?" asked Harwell, unable to contain himself any longer. "My many encounters with the little creatures have led me to believe that they are three in number. But I have never actually set eyes on them. How many, tell me?"

Without lifting the lid any higher, and still without any change of expression, Sarah prodded a bony forefinger at the inside of the box and did a quick calculation. "Four, Harwell," she said. "I can count four."

Harwell hugged himself with glee. "*Four!* An unexpected bonus! I had thought three. And how are they, Sarah? What's their mood? A trifle fractious perhaps? Are they anxious, do you think, to be allowed out on to the table?"

"They are more anxious, I imagine to sample the wash-tub—"

"What?"

"There is nothing in here save two pairs of those brats' soiled stockings!" cried Sarah, her voice rising with anger as she threw back the lid of the boot-black box. Then, getting to her feet, she emptied the contents into her brother's lap.

It was true.

The box held nothing except two pairs of dirty stockings.

"I shall leave you to decide what to do with them, Harwell," Sarah continued. "When you are finally certified insane, brother, it would be only right and proper for me to share your padded cell. I should not have listened to one word of your idiocy concerning fairy folk! I am going to my bed. I shall have more to say on this matter in the morning. Good-night!"

Sarah Mincing picked up the oil-lamp and swept out of the room, leaving her brother slumped in his chair, unhappy, alone in the dark.

11

Ernest pulled back the curtains at the window and the early morning sunlight flooded into the bedroom.

"Hey!" said Emily, waking instantly and sitting up in bed. "You know what today is, don't you?"

" 'Course I do. It's seaside day. It's the day we're going down on to the sand."

Emily nodded eagerly. "I'm that excited!" she said. "I bet they are as well —" As she spoke, she leaned over, reached down underneath her bed and pulled out a large hat-box. "Did you sleep well?" she asked, taking off the lid. "Was it comfortable in there?"

The three Lilliputians had spent a very comfortable night indeed inside the luxuriously velvet-padded hat-box—but they were not going to admit it.

"It made a change," said Fistram, offhandedly.

"A little lacking in dignity perhaps," observed Spelbush.

"I have spent less comfortable nights, I suppose," said Brelca. "At least it wasn't full of biscuit-crumbs," she added, glowering at Fistram, "like that old boot-box."

"It's a good job you weren't inside the boot-box last night," Ernest said, peering under his own bed. "It's gone!"

"Are you sure that's where you left it?" asked Emily.

"Positive," said Ernest, nodding. "Somebody must have

been in here while we were asleep last night and pinched it."

"Who'd want to pinch an old boot-box?" asked Emily, puzzled. "Hey—that means our mucky stockings have gone as well. I put them in there."

"My dear little girl, it's as plain as a plumstone who stole the boot-black box—Harwell Mincing," said Spelbush, then turning to Fistram and Brelca he went on, "If Sarah Mincing is here, can Harwell Mincing be far away? That's the reason I decided it would be far safer to pass the night in the hat-box."

"No, it isn't!" retorted Brelca, tartly, tossing her head in Fistram's direction. "It was because *I* refused to spend one more night in a box that was full of *his* biscuit crumbs!"

"There's no need to be so bad-tempered about it, Brelca," replied Fistram. "If it had not been for my biscuit crumbs, we *would* have spent the night in the boot-black box—and where would that have left us now? You should both be very grateful for my fondness for biscuits."

"It had nothing whatsoever to do with biscuit crumbs," stormed Spelbush. "It was all because of my foresight and leadership!"

"Biscuit crumbs!" snapped Brelca, stamping her foot.

"Foresight and leadership!" cried Spelbush, puffing out his chest.

"Oh, do be quiet, both of you!" bleated Fistram. "I can barely hear myself think about breakfast!"

"If you don't shut up, all three of you," said Emily, "we shan't bring you any breakfast back from the dining room."

"If you don't behave," added Ernest, "we shan't take you with us down to the sea today."

Intent on their argument, the little people had quite

forgotten what was planned for them that morning. Now that they had been reminded of it, they stopped their quarrelling instantly.

"We're actually going down to the sea!" sighed Brelca, happily.

"At last!" added Fistram.

"And all thanks to my foresight and leadership," said Spelbush, quietly complimenting himself.

"More tea, anyone?" asked Mr Garstanton, brandishing the tea-pot and looking around the breakfast table.

Emily, Ernest and Millie dolefully shook their heads. Breakfast in Miss Mincing's boarding-house had not proved the happiest of meal-times, despite the fact that the children were soon to be taken down to the sands for the very first time. For one thing, the Garstanton group were the *only* guests in the gloomy building—for another, Harwell's skill with a frying-pan left a great deal to be desired.

Not that Mr Garstanton was aware that it had been Miss Mincing's brother who was responsible for the unappetizing mess on his plate. "Oh, come along—come along," said the old photographer with a sigh, trying to make the best of things. "It wasn't *too* bad a meal, surely? All right, admittedly the fried eggs were a trifle over-cooked—*and* the sausages just a shade under-done—*and*, yes, the porridge was a little lumpy—and, well, the toast was burnt, slightly—but this tea is excellent . . ." Mr Garstanton paused, sighed again, and then added, "Or at least it would be if the milk hadn't turned just the tiniest bit sour."

There was another unhappy silence around the table. It was Millie who was the first to find her tongue.

"If that Miss Mincing gives me another of 'er dirty looks," said the housemaid, looking towards the kitchen door, "I shall give 'er back a piece of my mind, just see if I don't!"

Mr Garstanton sighed a third time, louder and longer than before. Perhaps, he asked himself, coming back to stay at Miss Mincing's house had not been such a good idea after all?

But if Mr Garstanton, Millie and the children were unhappy at staying in the boarding-house, Sarah Mincing was equally unhappy at having them as boarders.

"There!" she observed with some satisfaction as she scrawled her signature on a sheet of paper at the kitchen table. "That's got shot of them—and good riddance to all four!"

"What's that, sister?" asked Harwell, who was scouring dirty pans at the kitchen-sink.

"Why—their account, of course," said Sarah. "I shall hand it to the fool of a photographer when next I go into the dining room. And after breakfast they can pack their bags and clear out."

"Sarah, you can't—you *mustn't*!" said Harwell, aghast at the very thought.

"Oh, but I can!" said Sarah. "And I *shall*!"

"Listen to me, sister," pleaded Harwell, wiping his hands on a tea-towel. "I admit that we failed last night in our attempt to get our hands on the cunning creatures —"

"Last night? If only it were just last night!" cried Sarah, sorrowfully. "But if you've failed once, Harwell Mincing, you must have failed a score of times!"

"All the more reason then, Sarah, why we must not stop now. Think of all the time and effort wasted. Consider the money that we've invested in this enterprise."

"You mean that *I've* invested," said Sarah with a scowl.

Sarah thought hard. It was true. She had financed her brother so many times that she had lost count of the money she had spent on his foolish pipedream. She could, of course, tot up the exact amount—for she had entered every single penny in her cash-book. But to consider the total cost would only depress her the more. And supposing that Harwell was one day proved right? What if there really were such things as miniature people? And supposing then that, one far-off day, Harwell *did* manage to achieve his heart's desire and capture these mannikins? And just suppose, Sarah considered to herself, that she was not around then to recoup her losses and share in the fortune?

"You *have* invested a great deal in the project, sister," said Harwell, who could read Sarah's thoughts as easily as he could read the horse-race fixtures. He realized that she was wavering in her decision to send the old goat and the brats and the skivvy packing. "And you shall have every penny back a thousandfold," he continued, pressing home his advantage. "Sarah, those brats have the cunning creatures concealed somewhere in this house. I swear to it. They hid them from us last night. Shall we allow two ragamuffins to get the better of us? No, I say! For as long as they are in this house, we have the chance to snatch them."

Sarah considered the possibility. "Very well," she said at last. "But as long as they are on holiday here, Harwell, your place is in this kitchen. If I'm to feed and board you, you must earn your keep."

Harwell sighed and nodded, sadly. He contemplated two weeks of potato-peeling and scouring pans. The prospect did not appeal at all. But if that was the price he must pay for the opportunity to make his fortune—so be it.

At least the battle of wits between himself and the little mannikins was not yet over.

Mr Garstanton, Millie, Emily and Ernest arrived at the top of the broad wooden steps that led from the promenade to the beach. Millie was carrying the children's shrimping nets while Mr Garstanton had a tartan travelling rug under one arm and a copy of his favourite magazine, *The Photographic Camera*, under the other. Emily was carrying two buckets and two spades while Ernest clutched the boot-black box.

They had found the box, complete with dirty stockings, on top of the dustbin outside the back door of the boarding-house—where Harwell Mincing had dumped it in his disappointment.

The children stood transfixed for a moment as they took in the glorious expanse of empty golden sand. Then, with a concerted whoop of joy, they ran down the steps and raced across the beach.

Inside the boot-black box, the three Lilliputians held on to the sides for safety as the floor jogged dangerously beneath their feet.

"Have a care there!" shouted Spelbush, as the box swung to and fro.

"It's no good, Spelbush," wailed Fistram. "They won't pay the slightest attention!"

"No consideration whatsoever for their elders and betters!" snorted Spelbush.

"Don't say that you weren't warned!" snapped Brelca. "Don't say that I didn't tell you! I said from the very beginning that we were wrong to get mixed up with giant children!"

The tide was out.

Emily and Ernest ran on and on across the loose sand towards where the greeny-blue waters lapped all along the edge of the beach.

Some time later, Mr Garstanton sat on his travelling rug engrossed in his magazine. Millie had taken off her boots and stockings and had lifted her skirts above her ankles to paddle in the sea. Emily and Ernest, happier than they had ever been before, were busy with the shrimping nets not far from a large, many-towered and turreted sandcastle they had built. The castle was decorated with seaweed and mussel-shells. There was a deep moat around the walls which had quickly filled with water when they had opened up a channel to the nearby water's edge.

" 'Ere, what a lark, eh?" called Millie, grinning over her shoulder. She had wandered along, testing her toes in the sea, for some twenty or thirty yards. "I dunno why you chose to build that there castle quite so close to the briny!" she shouted. "It'll get washed away as soon as the tide turns!"

"It doesn't matter!" Ernest called back at her.

"We *wanted* it close to the sea, Millie!" cried Emily.

"As close to the sea as possible," remarked Brelca who, together with her two companions, was standing on a sheltered sand-terrace on top of one of the sandcastle's towers, gazing out towards the horizon.

"If only for a little while," said Spelbush, softly. He filled his lungs with the salt air and then let out a slow sigh of satisfaction. "Isn't that the most delicious smell in the entire universe?" he said. "I hope you'll both believe me in the future—I said I'd get you to the sea and here we are!"

"I don't know what you've got to feel so pleased about, Spelbush," squeaked Fistram. "We're not back in Lilliput yet—*and* we're living in the same house as Harwell Mincing."

"What better place to be?" said Brelca. "Right where we can keep an eye on him."

"A plumstone for both the Mincings!" cried Spelbush, who was in one of his devil-may-care moods. "We've beaten him a score of times before—we'll get the better of him a score of times again!"

"More if needs be," declared Brelca.

"Precisely!" said Spelbush. "It all serves to add a touch of zest to life." He paused and peered out again across the rolling sea. "And one day, Fistram—one of these fine days—we'll be out there on a ship of our own and sailing home!"

"With the wind in her sails and her prow pointed at the horizon!" cried Fistram, catching the mood of his companions.

"One of these fine days . . ." agreed Brelca, adding, "But not *just* yet—I'm enjoying myself far too much!"

THE PHANTOM TOLLBOOTH
Norton Juster

"It seems to me that almost everything is a waste of time," Milo remarks as he walks dejectedly home from school. But his glumness soon turns to surprise when he unwraps a mysterious package marked "One Genuine Phantom Tollbooth".

Once through the Phantom Tollbooth, Milo has no more time to be bored, for before him lies the strange land of the Kingdom of Wisdom and a series of even stranger adventures.

"The story is always charmingly inventive - Jules Feiffer's drawings splendidly catch the spirit of it - and in some families I think it could become a well-thumbed classic."

Guardian

To order direct from the publishers, just tick the titles you want and fill in the order form on the last page.

CHARLIE MOON AND THE BIG BONANZA BUST UP

Shirley Hughes

When Linda, the children's librarian, asked Charlie, his cousin Ariadne, and his friend Dodger to help organise the Book Bonanza, she might have known there'd be trouble. For their involvement goes further than high jinks in the horse costume: soon they find themselves on the track of sinister thieves and plotters.

"Another hilarious story about the irrepressible Charlie and his friend."

Books for your Children

£2.25

To order direct from the publishers, tick the titles you would like and fill in the order form on the last page.

THE CHRONICLES OF NARNIA

C. S. Lewis

C. S. Lewis's wit and wisdom, his blend of excitement and adventure with fantasy, have made this magnificent series beloved of many generations of readers. The final book, *The Last Battle*, won the Carnegie Medal for 1956.

Each of the seven titles is a complete story in itself, but all take place in the magical land of Narnia. Guided by the noble Lion, Aslan, the children learn that evil and treachery can only be overcome by courage, loyalty and great sacrifice.

The titles, in suggested reading order, are:

The Magician's Nephew	£2.50
The Lion, the Witch and the Wardrobe	£2.50
The Horse and His Boy	£2.50
Prince Caspian	£2.50
The Voyage of the Dawn Treader	£2.50
The Silver Chair	£2.50
The Last Battle	£2.50

To order direct from the publishers, just tick the titles you want and fill in the order form on the last page.

THE BOX OF DELIGHTS
John Masefield

Kay was certain that the Punch and Judy man had something magical about him. His strange wooden box certainly did. Where did it come from? And who were the shadowy, menacing figures so determined to get it? Soon Kay found himself drawn into a world of wonder, magic and danger - and that Christmas was the most unusual, beautiful one he had ever known.

A thrilling adventure story for young readers. John Masefield's *The Midnight Folk* is also available in Lions.

The Box of Delights	£2.50
The Midnight Folk	£2.25

To order direct from the publishers, just tick the titles you want and fill in the order form on the last page.

THE LAST VAMPIRE

Willis Hall

"My grandfather was the last of the Draculas. I do change into a bat occasionally, but I wouldn't dream of sucking anyone's blood. As a matter of fact, I'm a vegetarian. I'm simply mad about oranges."

On a camping holiday somewhere in Europe, the Hollins family encounter rather more than they had bargained for. They find themselves involved in a hilarious adventure - which takes them deep into vampireland.

£2.75

To order direct from the publishers, tick the titles you would like and fill in the order form on the last page.

THE INFLATABLE SHOP

Willis Hall

This time the Hollins family have decided to take no risks with their annual holiday, so they decide to stay at the Sea View hotel in Cockleton-on-Sea. After a rather boring start, the holiday suddenly takes a turn for the better when son Henry steps inside Samuel Swain's shop, filled with inflatable boats, balloons and toys, and discovers that the proprietor has got into rather a muddle with his inflatable equipment...

£2.25

To order direct from the publishers, tick the titles you would like and fill in the order form on the last page.

DRAGON DAYS
Willis Hall

Another Hollins family holiday in Cockleton-on-Sea takes a peculiar turn when Henry is transported back in time to Camelot in the days of King Arthur. The wizard Merlin needs his help to save the dragons from extinction; he doesn't know that Henry's mother has come too...

"A very entertaining book with a sparkling text." *Junior Bookshelf*

£2.75

To order direct from the publishers, tick the titles you would like and fill in the order form on the last page.

All these books are available at your local bookshop or newsagent, or can be ordered from the publishers.

To order direct from the publishers, just tick the titles you want and fill in the form below:

Name:...

Address:...

....

Send to: Collins Children's Cash Sales,
         P. O. Box 11,
         Falmouth,
         Cornwall TR10 9EN

Please enclose a cheque or postal order or debit my Visa/Access card:
Credit card No:
Expiry date:

Signature:...

- to the value of the cover price plus:

UK: 80p for the first book, plus 20p per copy for each additional book ordered to a maximum charge of £2.00

BFPO: 80p for the first book, plus 20p per copy for each additional book.

Overseas and Eire: £1.50 for the first book, £1.00 for the second book, thereafter 30p per book.

Young Lions reserve the right to show new retail prices on covers which may differ from those previously advertised in the text or elsewhere.